Waltz in Happiness

NILAKSHI BORGOḤAIN

Waltz in Happiness

NIYOGI
BOOKS

Published by
NIYOGI BOOKS
D-78, Okhla Industrial Area, Phase-I
New Delhi-110 020, INDIA
Tel: 91-11-26816301, 26813350, 51, 52
Fax: 91-11-26810483, 26813830
email: niyogibooks@gmail.com
website: www.niyogibooks.com

Cover Design: Supriya Saran
Layout Design: Nihar Ranjan Das
Editor: Barnali Ojha

ISBN: 978-81-89738-85-3

Publication: 2011

Printed at: Niyogi Offset Pvt. Ltd., New Delhi, India.

For

Satya…Truth

Gautam (Jolly)…Happiness

Aishwarya…Beauty

And truth is beauty

and beauty is happiness…

Acknowledgements

I owe my deepest gratitude to several wonderful people who made it possible for me to write and publish *Waltz in Happiness*, my first novel.

I am grateful to Mr Nirmal Kanti Bhattacharjee, ex Editor, Indian literature, Sahitya Akademi, New Delhi and presently Director, Birla Foundation, New Delhi. Had he not categorically asked me to write a novel, I should not have thought it was possible. I owe him a debt of gratitude for prodding me to venture into this challenging world of novel writing. This book surely would not have been possible without his critical guidance.

Mrs Tultul Niyogi and Mr Bikash Niyogi of Niyogi Books enthusiastically appreciated *Waltz in Happiness* and generously offered to publish the book. I thank them for their contribution in infusing life to my manuscript in the form of a most attractive book.

Barnali Ojha, my dear editor, worked so sincerely and lost herself so completely in the story, that by the end of the final draft she was on first name terms with all the characters of the novel! Her undivided commitment and dedication to the manuscript is highly commendable.

I have to also mention and thank here Dr Mamoni Raisome Goswami, eminent writer from Assam and recipient of the

Sahitya Akademi Award and the Jnanpith Award. Her continuous encouragement has been a great inspiration.

My husband, Satya Borgohain has been very supportive of my interest in writing. This is a wonderful opportunity for me to thank him for his support.

And finally, to all my well wishers and friends who habitually greet me with the opening sentence, 'So, what are you writing now?' —thank you for making my writing so much a part of your lives.

Nilakshi Borgohain
Gurgaon, 2010.

Chapter 1

'Not possible Sir. This type of big cars are impossible to open from outside.' The parking lot attendant speaks in a resigned voice after trying earnestly for ten minutes to unlock the door with an old silver scale and a one-meter long copper wire.

'Is there a garage nearby?' Pranjal asks him.

'Sir, it's Sunday today. And it's late. There's no way you can get a mechanic now. It's best to ring up home and ask someone to come with the extra keys,' he suggests.

Pranjal lives alone. There is no one who can get the duplicate key without breaking into his apartment. It is pointless in his taking a taxi to Gurgaon to fetch the keys. He can drive back in his faithful old SUV, but the trip will take him more than a couple of hours.

He has to fly to Hyderabad early next morning. For that reason, he cannot leave the car in the parking lot and come to collect it the following morning. What a wretched end to a sumptuous Mexican dinner!

'*Bhaiya*, having some trouble?' he must be around thirteen. Tousled black hair, chocolate brown, meltingly innocent eyes.

A cheap, black canvas bag hangs on his left shoulder, bulging with figurines. He is carrying a few collectibles in his hands to display them.

'I forgot my keys inside the car. I've locked myself outside.' Pranjal looks at him. Assessing him.

'I know a mechanic. He's a friend. Lives right across the road,' the boy smiles.

'It's Sunday. Almost eleven o'clock… will you get him?' Pranjal eyes him hopefully.

'Sure, *Bhaiya*! I'll be glad to help you. I'll be back in a moment,' he is gone before Pranjal is able to articulate another word.

Pranjal looks around. The parking lot is swiftly clearing up with the diners heading home. However, there are a few cars still around. Connaught Place, the pulsating heart of Delhi, boasts of some fine dining restaurants. A young woman wearing a shiny maroon, tattered *lehanga choli*, carrying red balloons approaches him. Her carelessly worn attire amply exposes her scrawny, sunburnt, soiled body.

'*Sahib*, buy some balloons,' she waves the balloons towards Pranjal and smiles.

'No, I don't need any,' he responds curtly.

'I've got stuff,' she smiles slyly. 'Stuff to blow your mind away.'

'I do not need anything.' Pranjal glares at her.

'Move away! Didn't you hear what Sir said? He doesn't want anything.' Just when Pranjal was pondering about the course of action he should take, his helpful Samaritan is back. 'Good thing you didn't encourage her, *Bhaiya*. This one does *nasha* (drugs). Best avoid her. Here's Lakshman. He is a good mechanic.'

Lakshman is a lanky, light complexioned fellow around eighteen, with highlighted copper streaked wavy hair and green eyes. He takes one look at the car and emphatically states, 'Sir*ji*, this type of car cannot be opened. There's no option but to smash the rear side window. Then we can unbolt the lock with this wire.' He holds out the wire and skillfully bends it on the edge to facilitate maneuver the lock.

Pranjal feels sick. He had purchased the car barely two weeks back and now this. True, it is second hand. Yet it is as good as new. The previous owner, an old friend, had purchased it barely a year back. He had moved to Brisbane on a plump assignment. That is how Pranjal came to possess such a swanky set of wheels at a relatively reasonable price.

Although Pranjal had elevated himself to a monetarily enviable status, he is still cautious not to splurge. Along with his friends Rajvir, Rajpal and Rajeev, Pranjal worships money. They salivate over all that money can buy and wallow like the complacent rhinoceros luxuriating in a muddy bath on a humid afternoon in the wilds of Kaziranga, in the power those notes can command. Money, the friends believe, is the panacea of all ills of an individual, a family, even a nation.

Pranjal is eager to show off the car to Ruby, his fiancée.

'I've got a glass in my garage. I can fix it within ten minutes. No need to worry, Sir.' Lakshman speaks soothingly.

Pranjal is reminded of an old adage about a duplicate of everything being available for a price in Delhi.

'I'm not worried. But are you sure there is no other way to unlock the doors?' Pranjal asks to ascertain that breaking the window is indeed justified.

'Sir, you won't notice the difference between the new window and your original one. Trust me,' he looks at him intensely in the eye.

How many people has Pranjal trusted in this amazing city and how many, many times was he duped? He has lost count.

The very first day he arrived in Delhi, disaster struck. As he leaned against a pillar with his hand casually tucked in his jeans pockets, his gleaming new SLR camera, at that time his sole prized possession, stylishly dangled on his left shoulder. He contemplated whether to take an auto rickshaw or drive in the comfort of a taxi to the guesthouse. As he leisurely reached out to feel his precious camera, his palm encountered the pathetic belt of the camera. His camera was stolen. His carefully cultivated relaxed stance swung a hundred and eighty degree to a state of panic.

Even before stepping out of the railway station, he was robbed. He rued not paying heed to his mother's word of caution and remaining alert to his surroundings the moment he stepped out of his home. According to her, Delhi, in keeping with its multifarious metropolitan character, is a cheaters' paradise.

'And she hardly knew Delhi.' Pranjal thought. 'Ah, well, I have received a grand welcome to the city.'

He had promised not to trust anyone without double checking. However, this is an emergency. Pranjal has no option but to trust him. He asks the mechanic to get the glass from his garage.

Lakshman narrowly escapes splinters in his eyes as the glass shatters when he tries to force it out after diligently removing the plastic lining of the glass panel. Fragments of glass fall inside on the back seats as well. Thankfully, after another ten minutes of struggle, he becomes successful in unlocking the door.

Pranjal looks at the area of destruction with a heavy heart. Lakshman glances at him critically before taking out the new rear mirror from a packet to replace the broken glass.

Pranjal pays Lakshman.

Pranjal gives an extra fifty-rupee note in addition to buying the bagful of collectibles from the young chap who had come forward to help him. His Ma can always present them to her many ex-students who drop by to visit her. He then thoughtfully makes his way back to his lonely apartment.

He enjoys the drive to Gurgaon from Delhi. He generally takes the Mehrauli Road to Delhi and drives back via the brightly lit new National Highway No. 8.

The meandering Mehrauli Road offers an old-fashioned charm with fine majestic monuments evocative of the Muslim era dotting the landscape, blending ever so unobtrusively with the present panorama.

The sight of the majestic Qutub Minar never fails to uplift Pranjal's spirit, no matter how tough a day he has had. He had checked out the guidebook on Delhi and learnt that this victory tower is one of the finest stone towers and an important landmark in Delhi. Qutubuddin Aibak laid down its foundations in 1199 AD. His son-in-law and successor, Iltutmish, completed its construction. This stunning souvenir rockets up in its old-fashioned splendour, heralding the greatness of the mega city.

A little distance away dot the modern architectural marvels of a new India poised to take over the consumerist world—the glitzy malls.

The expressway, on the other hand, is a twenty-seven point seven kilometer stretch of cool driving experience. The stamp of modernity is heightened by the bold new skyscrapers—the offices of the multinational companies, visible on either sides of the expressway. Unlike the mutedly lit Mehrauli Road, this route is a riot of coloured lights. Red. Yellow. Green. Of cars speeding past. Dazzling signboards. Even the solar road studs glitter like little red disco lights on the edge of the road. The myriad bulbs in the airport flamboyantly illuminate the area as planes zoom above the cars. One can only marvel at the dizzying difference of the two eras in the two routes.

Pranjal observes that the metro railway tract constructed along the Mehrauli Road is almost nearing completion. Before long, the concept of a leisurely romantic drive will fade away a little further from the mainstream as those ancient relics of the past and give way to life in the fast lane of the contemporary period.

One reason Pranjal still avoids using the expressway during office hours is the tiresome wait at the toll gate. The wait somehow steals away half the pleasure of the smooth drive the route offers.

Pranjal has a spacious six bedroom apartment. He is confident Ruby will like the place. It is bright, airy, and strategically located facing a park. Ruby is a nature aficionado. Pranjal is confident that the sight of all those ornamental trees in the park will captivate her.

Ruby and Pranjal were introduced formally over lunch at her place. The grandeur of their estate overwhelmed him. In his state of mystified rapture, the beauty of everything and every being emerged matchlessly magnified. Pranjal nervously offered her the modest bouquet of roses from Ma's garden.

'Thank you. They're pretty,' Ruby said. The tenderness of her smile reflected in her warm brown eyes. 'This is the first time in my life I have received a bouquet of garden flowers from a man.'

Pranjal had deliberated long before gifting those flowers, deducing Ruby must be bored with receiving exorbitantly priced exotic flowers from her well-heeled suitors.

Between March and May, dangling sprays of the Indian Laburnum, *Cassia fistula*, bloom ornately in their bursting brilliance of golden hue, like the finest crafted earrings (by a jeweler from Bengal), from the face of the trees. In the hot weather, the splashes of gold fall like golden pendants, a sight that instantly revives one's spirits.

The Gul Mohur trees stylishly flaunt their bountifully adorned branches with the youthful green bipinnate leaves, until the flaming orange flowers bloom to highlight the colourful display. Graceful Jacaranda trees line all sides of the park. For the short period that they bloom between March and May, clusters of blue-mauve flowers borne profusely in loose pyramidal terminal panicles lend a lavender hue to the atmosphere.

Directly across the road is a Coral tree whose rich burgundy blooms against its bare branches exhibit a striking feature during January through March. Although the flowers are not fragrant, crows, mynahs, parakeets, babblers, bees and wasps crowd towards them transforming the tree from merely a pretty sight to a veritable life-sustaining wonder. Margosa, Frangipani and Peepal trees are also visible from the house.

Pranjal had worked hard to attain his present social status. His next step will firmly establish his foothold on the list of elite families. He calculated money and position are the pre-requisites to maintain an enviable position. It was also very clear to him that a wife from the correct background would swiftly elevate his position into another echelon.

Pranjal walks into his silent flat and goes to sleep. He is already missing Ruby without having spent even a day together. They became engaged this spring during his trip to Guwahati. Their marriage is scheduled to take place in the winters. Too long a wait for the impatient Pranjal.

Ruby is everything he had most likely since infinity conjured in his mind as his ideal woman. Suddenly, marriage was no longer an archaic conservative concept and spending all his days with Ruby until they were old and grey was all he could dream.

However, his mother cannot be rushed. After all those years of trying to induce him into holy matrimony, she now wants to celebrate her grand triumph with an extravagant wedding. Pranjal cannot disappoint her. After all, he has no siblings. Furthermore, how can he deny her this little pleasure when she has managed to find him a treasure like Ruby? Their marriage date, seventeenth December, is barely three months away. September is almost over.

Pranjal had first met Ruby at the open-air function of Assamese spring festival—*rongali bihu toli.* Ruby was dressed in traditional *muga mekhla sador* and was accompanied by her parents.

'Mrs Handique. *Namaskar*!' the Gohains greeted Ma.

'And this handsome young man must be your son, Pranjal. He looks as handsome as his father in his young days,' Mrs Gohain said. 'Mrs Handique, you and Pranjal must come over for lunch tomorrow. And I will not take 'no' for an answer.' Mrs Gohain never takes 'no' for an answer, not even from acquaintances she has not been in touch with for years.

'Thank you, Mrs Gohain. It will be a pleasure,' replied Mrs Handique. 'Ruby dear, meet my son, Pranjal. He is clever, witty and utterly selfish. Pranjal meet my favourite girl in the world, Ruby.'

Ruby gave him a half smile. He noticed her almost imperceptible flinch at her mother's high-handed behaviour, her involuntary shudder of distaste at her mother's overbearing remarks.

Pranjal shops like a *nizam* at Hyderabad. Pearls set in gold with diamonds, rubies, sapphires and emeralds. He has never before shopped for a woman. Not even for his dear Ma. Now he cannot stop himself from buying one set after another. 'This is all a good investment,' he consoles himself.

He can visualize the exquisitely crafted ornaments adorn Ruby's regal visage. He is behaving like a love-stricken teenager and is surprised to discover that he is enjoying every moment of it. Guilty after spending so much on a woman who is yet to become his wife, he purchases several less expensive sets for Ma and any other relations she might consider appropriate to gift on such a special occasion.

That evening Pranjal rings up Ruby. 'Hi! How are you doing?' he tries to sound calm. He is not about to let her know how excited he is to hear her voice. The realization that he has sunk so deep in an emotional pit cautions Pranjal that his doom is near and that he needs to tread carefully if he is to remain focused on his goal.

'I'm fine. How are you doing? How's Hyderabad? Must be hot, huh? Where are you staying? How was your flight? How is work?' Ruby shoots her rapid-fire questions.

'I'm missing you,' Pranjal blurts like a lovelorn idiot. Where was the suave, sophisticated man he prided himself of being?

'Perhaps we can visit Hyderabad after marriage?' she speaks hesitantly. Underneath all her brilliant intelligence and bravado, she is still a shy young woman.

A trait almost alien to him for all the women he had known never possessed it. There is an unpretentious aloofness in her carriage and an easygoing elegance in her conduct that generations of good breeding have bestowed upon her. Pranjal is quick to construe that even in sackcloth she would look regal.

Perhaps her mannerism attracted his attention to her in the first place. But he was in awe of her illustrious family background. He had accumulated everything money and intelligence could buy. An alliance with the Gohain family would seal his standing as a member of a family of eminence.

'I've been shopping. I hope you like my taste,' Pranjal says.

'You don't need to spend unnecessarily on me, Pranjal.'

'I'm not a rich man like all the other guys you must have met. But I hope you will accept my humble token of love.'

'Oh, Pranjal! I've always known that I would choose to marry a self-made man—someone whom I can respect.'

'And you're the woman I have been waiting for all my life.' Pranjal mused monogamy has never sounded so romantic. The thought acts as a cleansing astringent in scrubbing the dirt from his ulterior-motive.

Chapter 2

The day Pranjal reaches home (no matter how many houses he has in as many different places, this house where he grew up, where he still has his old room with all his childhood paraphernalia, will always remain a home for him), he is confronted with a new chapter in his life pregnant with expectation. The unusual flurry of activities in their serenely quiet home corroborates this reality. All around, there is an expectant energy of a new beginning in the atmosphere.

He reaches home well in time for lunch. Ma looks flushed with excitement. She is delighted to see him. It is written in her eloquent dovelike eyes, spread over her wide smile and painted the rosiest red over her golden cheeks.

'You look happy.' Ma says, hugging him in the warmth of her embrace. Her hand as she gently pats his cheek is as soft as the tender touch of a butterfly. Her white cotton *mekhela sador* with a simple blue border enhances her fair beauty. She never needed makeup to enhance her looks. The pink roses of excitement on her cheeks lend colour to her waning complexion, infusing life.

'And you look positively elated,' Pranjal beams.

Ma smiles again. For a woman who maintains an impassively expressionless countenance, she is having a tough time masking her happiness. 'Go and take a shower,' she smiles. 'You must be hungry. I'll lay the table.'

'I am famished,' Pranjal agrees. 'I will be down in ten minutes.' He takes two steps at a time to climb up the twelve steps of the staircase that lead to the bedrooms upstairs. He opens his bedroom door with great expectations. His eyes fly to the parcel brightly wrapped in electric blue (his favourite colour) hand made paper placed on his desk. He feels bubbling within him the same excitement he had experienced as a ten year old as he swiftly unpacks the gift.

This is a family tradition. Ever since he was a ten year old, Ma had a little present gift wrapped for him. Everyday, when he returned home from school he rushed up to unwrap the gift. Some days it would be a book he wanted to read, a fancy pen or even a useful thing like a tennis ball. The effort she took to wrap up the gift made all the difference. Every time he unpacked a gift, no matter what the gift was, the day turned special for him.

It is an old mariner's compass, the brass polished to a gleaming golden colour. It works perfectly.

'I am a little undecided Ma. I can't seem to positively ascertain which course I should apply for my engineering degree—electronics and communications or information technology?'

'I don't know for sure if I should take up the government job or should work with the multinational company.'

'Ma, I am a little unsure. I hope I am going in the right direction.' Pranjal said to Ma after his engagement.

Yes, he is always weighing his options, testing her patience to the utmost during their brainstorming sessions, mulling over the pros and cons of every situation before arriving at a logical conclusion. 'Meditate on this compass when in doubt about the directions you need to take in your journey of life,' she had written in her fine artistic handwriting.

Pranjal recognizes it is her unique manner of gently reminding him that she will not be present to guide him in the decisions he makes in the future. Marriage, she emphasized, is a perfect dish between two persons. The interference of a third person only spoils it.

Pranjal takes a quick shower and rushes down to the dining room to indulge in a feast fit for a prince. Fluffy, snow white, piping hot steamed rice served with his favourite accompaniments. Fresh, thick slices of succulent *Rohu* fish fried in mustard oil and simmered in a tangy tomato gravy garnished with juliennes of fresh ginger from the Garo Hills. *Ilish* fish from the river Padma in Bangladesh, steamed in a rich golden yellow paste of freshly ground mustard seeds and turmeric to which she adds a splash of raw mustard oil, juliennes of fresh ginger and garnishes with a generous handful of bright green coriander leaves.

There is one of her signature fish dishes, *Chital* fish crisply fried and cooked in a sweet sauce of fried red onions, sugar, carabola (star fruit), turmeric, salt, ginger paste, bay leaves and sultans that were made plump and juicy by being soaked in water for a few minutes. There is an array of small fried fishes garnished with pickled bamboo shoot and chillies while still hot to infuse the flavour of the pickle into the fish and create a spicy treat.

A tomato chutney made with jaggery compliments the meal. The jaggery is a treasured delicacy prepared from dates in the Hooghly district and annually brought for them by the Chatterjee family. They unfailingly bring *khejurer gur* for the Handiques on their return trips from their hometown in Howrah every winter.

There is copper red fried pumpkin flowers dipped in a light batter of flour, turmeric and mildly spiced with fresh herbs, tender pumpkin leaves coated with a crunchy batter of rice powder, succulent slices of fried eggplants—brinjals delicately flavoured with turmeric, salt and cumin seeds. This platter of vegetable savouries wet Pranjal's appetite as he starts munching them with the tangy garlic mint chutney, while waiting for Ma to slice the garden fresh luscious cucumber salad.

Mealtimes with Ma are Pranjal's most cherished moments of contentment. Not because they always indulge in an elaborate multi cuisine affair but because even the most basic food is served with so much affection. Perhaps it is this sense of sublime fulfilment, which he recaptures every time he prepares food, that he so enjoys cooking.

'Now, tell me how you are feeling.' Ma asks sitting on the sofa in the drawing room, taking a sip of lemon tea.

Pranjal is contemplating on his cup of lemon tea. A fragrant sliver of rich green lemon stylishly swims in the mild red tea served in a white porcelain tea cup. He has been waiting for her to return from the kitchen after rinsing the dishes and stacking them in the dishwasher.

'I guess a little apprehensive. I hope I can make Ruby happy,' he responds.

'What are you apprehensive about?' Ma asks.

'I don't know. I figure I am worried about the fact that I have been living alone for so long. I could prove to be an insufferable selfish oaf to live with,' Pranjal replies.

'You'll manage. Are you sure you are actually not worried about losing your independence?' Ma asks.

'She knows me better than I know myself,' Pranjal thinks. 'After all, I am her son—a son she has brought up all by herself ever since I was a ten year old. She knows that I prize my independence just as she treasures hers.'

'I know Ruby will never suffocate you with her presence. Although, the two of you will be quite inseparable, I can tell,' Ma says.

'Are you sure?' Pranjal desperately needs her reassurance. Decisions, responsibilities… all scare him.

'Positive.' Ma smiles. 'This is a new chapter in your life, Pranjal. Start it with a positive attitude. There can be moments when you may think you love Ruby less; there may be days when you will wish to be alone. Bear in mind never to cut off communication. A relationship is based as much on emotional and intellectual compatibility as on a physical one. As long as you remember that, you will do fine.'

'Yeah,' he responds thoughtfully.

'Do you still confide in Anita?' Ma asks.

There she does it again. There is not a thought in his mind that remains a secret from her.

'No Ma, I don't confide in her. We are just colleagues now. It's been almost eight years now since the proposal. We merely exchange formal office pleasantries occasionally. Ma, what I felt for Anita was nothing like what I feel for Ruby. I never wanted to spend my life with Anita. I knew right from the start that we would remain simply friends,' Pranjal explains.

'But Anita didn't. She loved you. She had hoped you would grow to love her one day,' Ma says. 'You cannot wish problems away, Pranjal. You have to grow up someday and learn to solve them like a man.'

'Ma, was it my fault I never fell in love with her? I never lied to her or led her on,' Pranjal counters.

'No, you didn't lead her on. On the other hand, even when I pointed out to you that she was in love with you, you refused to acknowledge it. Perhaps if you had distanced yourself from her back then, she won't have felt quite so badly let down,' Ma says.

'I always treated her like a friend. Honestly, Ma, we were in college together. She was just a friend. We never even dated!' he argues.

'But you did drink endless cups of coffee together… and discussed your dreams. Your attention must have led her to believe you harboured feelings for her.' Ma reminds Pranjal.

'I discussed my dreams and she would tell me her ambitions. She never featured in my dreams. So it should have been clear to her that I was not interested in her. Plus, her Dad always took us out to dinner whenever he was in town. They treated me like family,' he explains.

Ma looks at him meaningfully, stating the obvious with her silence. The sound of silence has always communicated to her and she communicates so much with her silence. 'It pays to bear in mind always to deliberate over in all situations from the other person's point of view as well. In fact, I would say it is as important to discern the thoughts of the person we are interacting with as it is to know our own mind,' Ma says.

How Pranjal wished Anita had not fallen in love with him. They could have remained friends. Still, when she proposed to him and he refused in the politest manner he knew, she swore she would make him suffer. She started work immediately after graduating from engineering college, while he completed his MBA. Coincidently, last year, she joined the company where he was working. The disturbing thought was that she was not in a relationship.

'I've mentioned Anita to Ruby,' Pranjal proclaims.

'Good,' Ma says. 'That reminds me, you are taking Ruby out for a romantic ride and dinner on the river Brahmaputra. The name of the steamer is 'Eastern Enchantress.' I know the name sounds cheesy. Even so, believe me she is beautiful. Mr Chatterjee's son, Abhijit, owns it. Abhijit is now a well-established businessman.'

Mr Chatterjee is Ma's colleague. He is the music teacher who sings the sweetest Rabindra *sangeets* and recites Tagore's poetry with a passionate zeal. He used to read poetry to Pranjal when he was in college. Pranjal still remembers his recitation of Tagore's 'The last Farewell'—*Shesher Kabita*, in Bengali. His fervent recital in that sweet lilting language lent a profundity to the beautiful poem in Pranjal's young mind. And he was hooked on Tagore and Bengali literature, not to forget the *khejurer gur*—jaggery prepared with dates, which Mr Chatterjee brought back from Kolkata.

'I guess I should fix up the time with Ruby,' Pranjal says.

'You are going to pick up Ruby at six,' Ma answers.

'Six o'clock! It's past four now. Are we going out for dinner or tea?' Pranjal asks.

'Don't you want to watch the sunset while sailing on the Brahmaputra?' Ma asks. 'Remember, the sun sets early here.'

'Thanks, Ma.'

'You're welcome. Don't forget this is your last outing together before your marriage. You are not to go out with each other from tomorrow till you are married.' Ma reminds him. 'Now go to your room and try to get some rest.'

Pranjal reaches Ruby's palatial bungalow driving Ma's relic an ancient Ambassador she refuses to part with, turning down all his attempts of presenting her with a new car of her or his choice. She rarely uses the vehicle, as she prefers walking.

According to Ma, if people walk to work, there will be no need for them to labour in the gyms and waste time and energy. In addition, imagine the amount saved on fuel and our contribution towards a healthier environment. For a woman who is nearing fifty, she sports a figure even a twenty year old would aspire. Yes, she definitely has a point.

Ruby is strolling in the garden, wearing a sea green chiffon top and cream cotton trousers. This year, winter is pleasantly mild. She looks stunning. As she smiles at him, Pranjal fails to respond. She has this effect of getting him all wired up.

'Hi!' Ruby's smile widens.

'Hi!' He fumbles back to the car and gets out the bouquet of blushing red roses he had brought for her. It strikes him that set against the background of the flowers in the garden, she herself looks like a lovely flower—an elegant, unusually coloured daffodil.

'For you.' Pranjal mentions redundantly, giving her the flowers. As an afterthought he adds, 'You look lovely.'

'Thanks,' she smiles. Pranjal observes she is smiling a lot. Happiness is floating around. 'Shall we go and meet my parents?'

'Aha, hullo, young man!' Mrs Gohain exclaims. Mrs Gohain is a very fashionable, very plump and a very confident woman. She comes from an elevated middle-class family. Her father who was the son of a tea garden owner was himself an extra assistant commissioner in the state government. Despite her background, Mrs Gohain is a petty-minded person whose world revolves around her beauty, her status and herself.

One could well be puzzled to observe a person of Mr Gohain's calibre so passively refrain from objecting to Mrs Gohain's vanity. Until one learns that Mr Gohain has a past, of which he is deeply repentant—his youthful dalliance with Mrs Gohain's cousin. Although the cousin moved on, married and lived a life of her own, Mr Gohain continued to be ashamed of his indiscretion. This guilt made him bow extra low when his wife reminded him of his transgression.

Mrs Gohain never let him forget his little misadventure. After deriding and belittling him in front of her many brothers and sisters, she would grandly announce how she forgave him and sacrificed her life for the sake of the girls—Pearl and Ruby.

Mr Gohain would cringe in shame and promise himself that he would try harder to erase the recollection of that bitter episode from her memory. What was beyond his understanding was that Mrs Gohain guarded his misdemeanour as a most prized possession to use to exercise maximum control over him.

'So, how was your flight?' Mrs Gohain asks Pranjal.

'Very pleasant. Thank You,' Pranjal answers.

'You look handsome. You would have made a better match with my elder daughter, Pearl. She is the beauty of the house. She resembles me.' Mrs Gohain could be most blasé while talking about her own beauty. 'Unfortunately, we had to marry her off early due to the deluge of proposals we were receiving for her. She is an absolute dream, any man would be proud to show her off as his wife. Ruby here is the quiet types.'

'Then we shall be in perfect harmony,' Pranjal counters. 'I am the peaceful types myself.'

'Why don't you stay for tea? We have important matters to discuss with you,' Mrs Gohain invites.

'Another day Moromi (darling),' Mr Gohain finally speaks extending a hand to greet Pranjal. 'Now let them go and enjoy themselves. Good to see you, son.'

'Thank you very much, Sir,' the warmth of his firm handshake reassures Pranjal.

Mr Gohain's father owned a small teashop. The family had no farmland save a small plot that housed their miserable hovel and two emaciated cows. Ever since he was a little boy, the rich people in their gleaming white Ambassador cars, who stopped by to drink tea in his father's stall, had fascinated Mr Gohain. The stall was at a railway crossing and when the gates closed down for almost a quarter of an hour for the trains to pass, restless passengers from vehicles would disembark and drink tea to refresh themselves and generally pass time. During summers the green coconut (*dab*) water seller, who sat by his father's stall, made more money. But fortunately for Mr Gohain Senior, tea is a year-long favourite brew for the people of Assam.

During summers, Mr Gohain would collect the paper napkins and tissue papers the *memsahibs* from the car threw out of their window after dabbing the sweat from their face. As he neatly flattened the crushed napkins and folded them, sometimes he would notice pink and red lipstick smudges on them. Their colour would send a shiver of thrill through his scrawny adolescent body. No woman he knew wore lipstick.

Mr Gohain worked very hard to move up to his social position. He studied consistently hard, won scholarships and secured admission in the leading colleges of the country. From nobody, he finally became somebody.

His entry into the world of his dreams now necessitated a high-class wife to complete the picture. Borokha a.k.a. Moromi Baruah was a perfect foil to the society he wished to step into. Borokha had studied up to class X and refused to study further. Her parents were at their wits' end with a daughter who spent the entire day grooming herself and refused to learn or do anything else to improve herself as an individual.

Chapter 3

Eastern Enchantress is a gleaming silver beauty in the blue waters of the Brahmaputra, as they reach her. It is relaxing to leave behind the hectic pace of the city and set sail on the wide expanse of the great river.

'See that emerald blob!' Ruby says, pointing out to the Peacock Island. 'Shall we go and light a *diya* in the temples? It's beautiful in there.'

The island houses the temples of Umananda, Chandreshkar and Hargavri. Pranjal is by no means religiously inclined and so has never ventured to the island so far. Although, the serpentine row of boats carrying pilgrims during *Shivratri,* celebrated annually around March, has always fascinated him.

If he happens to be at home during the great night of Lord Shiva—*Mahashivratri,* he cruises across on a country boat from Kachari Ghat and surrenders himself to the languid pace of life in North Guwahati. He sits on the secluded tranquillity of the banks of the Brahmaputra and watches Umananda Island illuminate with light and life.

They return to the steamer after lighting a *diya,* without waiting to explore around the island because dusk is setting in swiftly.

'I'm not a deeply devout individual, Pranjal.' Ruby volunteers this bit of information abruptly. 'I mean I'm really not into rituals and ceremonies. In my view, complicated practices in a religion restrict our spiritual growth. I believe the purpose of religion is to set us free to embrace all without bias.'

'That's profound belief for a twenty-one year old.' Pranjal smiles at her earnest conviction.

'Twenty-three. I am serious Pranjal. I have the greatest respect for all faiths because all religions ultimately teach us one truth. However, I refuse to remain bound by meaningless customs and traditions. I pray every day but I hesitate to identify myself a Hindu, Muslim, Christian or Buddhist, for I believe in the good of each religion and discard the doctrines I find constrictive to my growth as an individual.'

'Ma taught me to break all the old rules that my conscience revolted against. She took pains to sensitize me to the notion that our faith should be beyond any one religion. She has always emphasized on the spirituality aspect for a more fulfilling life, rather than on blindly subscribing to rituals. You don't need to worry too much about rites and ceremonies as long as we have the strength to listen to our inner voice,' Pranjal assures her.

Yet even as he speaks, a heavy shroud darkens his clear and happy mind, mocking him… were spirituality and dishonesty ever companions? How dishonest had he become over the years? Could he still claim to maintain his spiritual side? He brushes the nagging thought aside as one would an irritating housefly trying to feast on and spoil a perfectly scrumptious slice of chocolate cake. If he has chosen Ruby over Anita because of her family's exclusive eminence, he has committed no great sin. After all, he has checked out the complete package—looks, education, character and background. And as far as the question of social standing goes, Ruby stands right up the societal ladder whereas Anita's station could be well-ranked at the starting step.

Anita's father retired as an assistant from a private firm. One discrepancy in their society Pranjal was well-acquainted with was the snob value attached to a family name. One may make truckloads of money, but minus the additional qualification of an illustrious lineage, one is still not embraced within the coveted ranks of lofty folks.

Pranjal had always wanted to erase that offending smirk off the face of his cousin, Kartik, who insisted on referring to Pranjal as his 'poor cousin.' All because Kartik's mother had married into a well-known family while Pranjal's father was a farmer's son. Pranjal believed that marrying Ruby would eliminate this bias and put him at par with Kartik. After all, there are very few people who do not know of the great Mr Gohain, Ruby's father.

Pranjal's present dominant craving is to attain an enviable social equilibrium as the cherry on the cake of educational qualification, money and a good profession he had so far single-mindedly consolidated. One could very well concede that he methodically accomplished all his actions to fulfil this one aspiration of his.

'I always figured I would have a pretty hard time finding a man who shared my radical views. I'm glad we met, Pranjal! Our elemental perception of life is analogous. Life is good!'

Ruby's golden beauty looks heavenly against the flaming orange background of the setting sun and the breeze caressingly fanning her hair that fall heavily like coffee brown *muga* silk strands on her shoulders. Pranjal does not need to make a great effort to brush aside his uneasy thoughts.

A waiter brings a silver tray with tea and snacks.

'We'll serve ourselves. Thank you,' Pranjal says. He does not want anyone intruding on their precious moments together. The steward inclines his head and withdraws.

'One teaspoon sugar?' Ruby asks as she concentrates on pouring the refreshing aromatic hot brew into the cups. Pranjal inclines his head, watching her graceful conduct. A quality of timeless serenity in her presence makes him believe that he will forever be at peace with her.

'This is breathtaking!' Ruby declares watching the brilliant hues of the twilight sky as they sip tea and eat from the assortment of savouries and snacks.

'Absolutely breathtaking!' his glance lingers on her face.

'Stop teasing.' Ruby is quiet for a second. 'Do you know there are many romantic legends woven on the river Brahmaputra?'

'There are? As far as I know this is one deceptive river. So magnificently calm to view yet it ravages the valley every year with ruthless hunger,' Pranjal remarks. 'Tell me what tales you know about the Brahmaputra. Tell me why is it called the red river?' he enjoys listening to her.

'It is said that Agni, the fire God, once begged the Kshatriya king, Kartaviryarjuna, for food. The king allowed him to take as much as he wanted from his vast territory. Agni went on a rampage, burning forests and mountains. He even consumed the ashram of the sage Apava who was performing penance deep inside one of the forests.

'The enraged sage cursed the kshatriyas. An incarnation of Mahavishnu, named Parasuram, he said, would be born into the family of the Bhargavas who would descend on the earth to destroy the arrogance of the kshatriyas.

'It was in the Brahmaputra that Parasuram bathed, washing away his sins after annihilating the kshatriyas. The puranic belief is that he went around the world eighteen times to massacre the kshatriyas. The river was then known as Lauhitya (bathed), as it was believed to be, with the stains of blood in Parasuram's body.' Ruby concludes her tale.

'Very imaginative! Tell me how come Brahmaputra is a male river,' Pranjal urges. Despite his cynicism towards mythology, Ruby's matter-of-fact tone captures his interest to acquaint himself with more folklore.

'The story of Brahmaputra, son of Brahma, the creator of this world according to Hindu mythology, is mentioned in the ancient text, the Kalika Purana. According to this text and the Puranic Encyclopedia by Vettam Mani, there once lived a sage named Santanu, with his charming wife Amogha,' begins Ruby.

'One day, Lord Brahma visited the ashram of Santanu. Amogha received the guest with all due reverence, as her husband was not at home. Fascinated by her welcome, the god impregnated her,' Ruby continues.

'Wow! Fast work!' Pranjal smiles disbelievingly.

'It is a story Pranjal. I didn't just make it up. Anyway, unable to bear the divine pregnancy, she deposited the celestial gift in the waters flowing through the valley of the Yugandhar Mountain. From then on, it became a place to take a holy bath.' Ruby narrates.

'Fantastic.' Pranjal mutters, overcome, as he is with as immense an ardour as the great god himself. He kisses her.

Chapter 4

Their wedding is a traditional affair, performed in Thai Ahom *choklong* ceremony. Pranjal feels like they have journeyed a full circle. Both Ruby and he has travelled the world, studied at various metropolises. Yet, when it came to marriage, they had strangely found each other in their own city. However, as neither had spent a very long time at a stretch in Guwahati, it was hardly surprising that they had never met before.

Their marriage is a three-day-long affair. On the day of the *joron*, when Pranjal's family set out to the bride's place, he becomes rather restless. He and Ma have managed to fill two massive red suitcases with finery and ornaments for Ruby. Ma has added her own *Doog doogi, Dhol biri, Bana, Jon biri* and *Loka paro* sets and a magnificent *gaam kharu* along with the jewellery sets and *saris* he has amassed from Delhi, Varanasi, Kolkata, Chennai and Hyderabad. The *mekhela sador* sets are all from Sualkuchi. Baishya *da* specially wove the traditional designs. There are several sets in contemporary style as well.

Ma and Pranjal travelled to the sleepy village of Sualkuchi where almost all the families are involved with the Assam silk business one way or the other. From that lovely village they purchased Ruby the main wedding—white *pat* silk *mekhela sador* set, the stunning pattern was woven in golden thread.

Sualkuchi is barely thirty-two kilometres from Guwahati, so they choose to drive Ma's Ambassador car for the trip. They cross the Saraighat Bridge. The famous Battle of Saraighat was fought in 1671 between the Mughals and the Ahoms. Led by the courageous Lachit Borphukan, the Ahoms overpowered the mighty Mughal army.

An interesting folklore, *Dehkot koi Momai Dangor Nohai*—about how General Borphukan chopped off his maternal uncle's head when the latter, who was in command of the army, allowed the men to rest awhile their tired bodies—was Pranjal's favourite bedtime story. During the preparations for the Battle of Saraighat, Borphukan got a fortification (*garh*) constructed overnight and engaged his uncle to supervise the project.

Pranjal grew up insisting Ma to tell him the same story every night before he went to sleep. When the soldiers witnessed the nephew ruthlessly behead the uncle, despite being tired they immediately forsook their rest and resumed their work fearing their lives. After all, if a nephew did not hesitate in beheading his uncle, could he be expected to spare the soldiers? Remains of the *Momai Kota Garh,* earthen fort where the uncle was executed, are still visible by the Guwahati University campus in Assam. Borphukan's unqualified commitment to his duty never ceased to arouse Pranjal's youthful imagination.

Although the Ahom army was much weaker than the Mughal army, by their brilliant use of terrain, guerrilla tactics, military intelligence, psychological warfare and by exploiting the weakness of the Mughal forces, in particular its navy, the Ahoms prevented the attempt of the Mughals to extend their empire into Assam in the decisive Battle of Saraighat.

Pranjal's little heart would pump up in pride when Ma recounted the story of what a great hero Borphukan was.

After travelling through the picturesque countryside of cattle grazing on the green grass of the undulating plains and palm trees swaying against the banks of the Brahmaputra, they reach the silk village of Assam.

It is early morning, yet they hear the rhythmic sound of the looms. They drive around the village a bit, and then park their car in the compound of Mr Baishya's residence.

Mr Haresh Baishya is an acquaintance of Ma. Ma offers packets of chocolates and sweets she had brought from Guwahati to Mrs Baishya. Mr Baishya shows them around his house.

The cocoons are stacked in a room. The thread is spun, dyed and woven in the courtyard. There are twelve looms in his house. Apart from all the members of his family being involved in weaving, Mr Baishya also supports six women who live in a cottage owned by the Baishya family. These women are destitute whose dignity has been restored by the Baishya family who have arranged for them to earn a livelihood.

Soon Mrs Baishya invites them for breakfast. Their youngest son, eleven-year-old Chintu, brings out a *lota* (a vessel typically meant to contain water) and a sparkling white hand woven towel—*gamosa*, its border designed with *japees*—straw hats, in scarlet. They wash their hands with the water Chintu pours out from the *lota* and wipe their hands with the *gamosa*.

They enter the dining room, which has a wooden table covered with a green hand-woven tablecloth. The table is laden with *luci*, potato curry, and tomato chutney, a variety of rice flour *pethas*, coconut *laddus* and tea. Mrs Baishya keeps replenishing their plates with piping hot fluffed up round *lucies* prepared with flour as soon as they finish eating one.

'*Baidow* (elder sister), if you give me one more *luci*, I shall be too lethargic to proceed for our shopping spree.' Pranjal pleads with her to stop serving him more food.

'Nonsense. You are a young man! You should have a healthy appetite.' Mrs Baishya exhorts affectionately.

'She wishes to turn me into a nice rotund *luci*, I fear,' Pranjal muses.

Their stomachs very nicely satiated, they set out to make their purchases. With Mr Baishya by their side, they can only buy the very best pieces. The finest *mekhela sadors* are available here. They purchase a white *pat* silk three-piece *mekhela sador* and *riha* woven with the most exquisite floral design in gold thread all over the garment. This is the wedding attire, which their family will be presenting Ruby with during the *joron* ceremony along with the golden *muga* silk *mekhela sadors* and the *pat muga* saris.

Folding the attire lovingly, Mr Baishya tells Pranjal, 'Presenting your bride with this exquisite traditional attire to adorn herself with during the sacred wedding ceremony, you promise to always respect her as a human being.' He pats Pranjal's back.

That nasty niggling shroud attacks with piercing precision, entrapping Pranjal's bright and clear mind, threatening to swathe his multi-coloured dreams.

He shakes his head. He is finding it increasingly hard to retain the nonchalant demeanour he had cultivated as an urban dweller. A little lying, an occasional bout of dishonesty to clinch a deal, never disturbed him with the slightest tinge of guilt.

This time, Pranjal found himself uncomfortable in his careless, deceptive conduct.

'Are you okay, Pranjal?' Ma asks.

'Fine, Ma. Just a little tired, I guess. Must be the excitement,' Pranjal speaks smoothly.

'You need rest. We'll be home soon.' There is concern in Ma's voice.

While bidding them farewell, Mr Baishya fills up the dickey of their Ambassador with bananas and vegetables from his garden. Pranjal's trepidation that their car will break down midway is unfounded as the old engine demonstrates its sturdy build. They reach home safely.

The splendid gifts impress the bride's family. Even Mrs Gohain's friends who so berated her on her choice of a suitable groom for Ruby admire the fine collection. Ma also gave a gigantic fish Mr Chatterjee's fishmonger had caught from the Brahmaputra in the early hours of the morning. Fish is an auspicious omen in this part of the country. Fish is even distributed to friends and relations when a son is born.

Mrs Gohain and Ma obviously have very little in common. Ma is a woman who has struggled all her life, yet she never complains about anything. She has the perfect recipe for making lemonade with all the lemon life bombards her.

On the other hand, Mrs Gohain has the ability to complain nonstop on a minor inconvenience. A major nuisance in her life is her daughter Ruby.

Ruby is everything Mrs Gohain is not. She is independent, intelligent and passionately involved in her work. She is equally at home conversing with the heads of the state as she is chatting with illiterate starved families devastated by the floods. Contrarily, Mrs Gohain is allergic to any person beneath her in the social hierarchy.

Most of the functions in a marriage takes place in the bride's house. The groom has to make do with a reception in his home before he sets out with his entourage for the bride's place for the wedding ceremonies.

Generally, the groom arrives at the bride's home in the best car. Before the advent of the motor vehicle, grooms made that journey on elephants or bullock-carts or even on foot, if they could not afford the venerable elephants and cows. Pranjal chose to make this cherished journey in his mother's gleaming white Ambassador. It stood out rather impressively as a vintage car amidst all the sedans of their relatives.

Two of Ruby's very muscular uncles lift and carry Pranjal bodily to the *mandap* where the traditional ceremony will take place as soon as the bride arrives. Fortunately, during his plight whilst being thus manhandled, Pranjal has the presence of mind to clutch on to his *dhoti* to save himself from the embarrassment of it falling off.

Once seated, he concentrates on the hundred and one *diyas* (earthen lamps) strategically placed over the hundred and one lotus petals artistically drawn with all the colours of life by the *deos* (priests). Beneath each *diya* is a coin to be offered along with other gifts to the poor the following morning. Ruby's best friend, Poornima, leads her to the *mandap*. As she sits down beside Pranjal, he tries to get a glimpse of her.

The exquisite golden design woven in the white *pat* silk *riha* (veil) demurely covers her face. This simple act heightens the sense of mystery in her new avatar as a bride and Pranjal finds himself impatient with the desire for a glimpse of her. He stares at her as she stretches out her delicate hand towards him as instructed by the *Deodhai Phukan*. He looks spellbound at her face warmly reflected like the moon with the luminosity of the hundred and one lit *diyas* that shine like the stars. His eyes meet hers. The sound of laughter is too loud to ignore.

'Well now, young man, if you have quite done with gazing at your bride, shall we proceed with the formalities? You have the rest of your life to look at her. Now take out the ring you have for her. The poor girl has been waiting with her hand stretched out long enough,' *Deodhai Bor Phukan* says.

'Sorry.' Pranjal fumbles to extricate the infuriatingly tiny jewellery box containing the precious ring from his *kurta* pocket. Sandeep, his school friend, who had committed to be by his side as his best man during the wedding appeared to have vanished. Much later, Pranjal catches a glimpse of him steadily getting drunk on the expensive scotch and whisky doled out liberally.

Ruby's father, as per the ceremony, hands over the *hengdan*, the traditional sword, to Pranjal. The *hengdan* is a single edged sword with a long handle. The handle and the scabbard are engraved in gold. Handing over the *hengdan* is a symbolic representation of formally acknowledging the groom as the bride's protector. Pranjal trembles as the metallic heirloom on his hands emphasizes the truth that Ruby's honour is now in his hands.

Their wedding scriptures are in Thai Ahom script, a language no longer commonly spoken in Assam. *Sri Phukan* and *Sri Bor Phukan* were both professors at the University before they took to performing marriage ceremonies as a full time occupation. They are the *Deodhais* or the priests who conduct the necessary rituals. They are equally conversant in Assamese and Thai Ahom languages. Thus, they translate every verse that they chant in Thai Ahom into Assamese so that the bride and groom understand exactly what they are letting themselves in for by agreeing to the marriage.

The wedding ceremony is a long, long affair. First is the exchange of vows and garlands; then follow the rules and guidelines laid down for the conduct of a happy married life. Finally, the fun and games devised to determine who would have the last word in their married life. Positioned between them rests a cane basket filled with fragrant *joha* rice. Their respective rings lay well hidden in the rice. The one who is able to find the ring first wins the game. Pranjal purposely lets Ruby win every game. He has already won his prized trophy in her.

That night, they bring Ruby home only for a few minutes. All his hopes of a wedding night dash to the ground when he learns that it is customary for the bride to return to her mother's home for the night. Mr Gohain reasons it is best that Ruby leave her parental home after the reception the following night. Ma agrees that the proposal is ideal, as it will give the tired bride an opportunity to rest.

The reception is a fashionably grand affair with all the very important people of the state in attendance. Mr and Mrs Gohain personally ensure that every guest is attended to with the greatest hospitality. Customarily, it is of paramount importance to feed and treat every guest with utmost courtesy, irrespective of his or her social standing.

If the hosts fall short in their responsibility of treating each invitee with the greatest politeness, it is considered a transgression that is tantamount to an inauspicious beginning of a life together for the newly wed couple. Hence, an army of relations, strictly assigned to various responsibilities, look after the guests.

Mr and Mrs Gohain introduce every guest to Ruby and Pranjal. They personally accept every gift. Little Tina, Ruby's niece, stands alongside her with a *bota* of fragrant *suparie*, *pan* and Ruby offers the guests the tiny pieces of sweetened betel nut from the bell metal platter after personally accepting the gifts.

When Mrs Gohain occasionally tries to gloss over the introductions while introducing a person of lesser social eminence, Mr Gohain nattily takes over the introductions. It is easy to see how their marriage is a success.

He introduces Pranjal to his earlier office staff with as much warmth as he does his colleagues. Although he is retired, Pranjal doubts anyone from the various departments he served during his tenure has skipped the wedding. Mr Gohain has obviously generated an immense amount of goodwill during his service life.

'Aaha, Mrs Handique as you can see, like her mother, our Ruby is used to immense luxury. I do hope Pranjal will be able to maintain her in a similar style,' Mrs Gohain says to Ma.

'Mrs Gohain, Pranjal also has an abundance of love for her. He will shower her not only with a profusion of material wealth but also with the warmth of his pure love for her,' Ma replies.

'Well as long as there is no undue interference from your side, I suppose they will be happy,' Mrs Gohain smiles slyly.

'No Mrs Gohain. There shall never be any interference from my side. As you are well aware, I have a very busy life of my own. You can put your mind to rest. The children shall be happy together,' Ma assures her.

Overhearing the exchange, Pranjal wants to go and tell Mrs Gohain, his brand new mother-in-law, to mind her manners. Except, he is the bridegroom with whom a constant flow of guests are shaking hands and congratulating.

Imagine attending a wedding and not being able to wish the bride and the groom a happy married life. No guest will ever forget such a slight his or her entire life. It will be most inappropriate for Pranjal to leave Ruby's side and tell Mrs Gohain exactly what is in his mind. Ma will never excuse such indiscretion.

Pranjal makes a mental note to bring up the matter later. No one is going to lecture his mother on her conduct with her family.

Of course, he completely forgets about the unpleasant dialogue between Ma and Mrs Gohain in the ensuing commotion. The next day they leave Guwahati for Gurgaon.

Chapter 5

'So, what do you think of your new home?' Pranjal asks eagerly. He had done up the flat with all the latest gadgets keeping in mind Ruby's requirements. He is keen on starting their life together perfectly. No loopholes dangling carelessly.

Ruby enters the doorway wearing a smile of wonder. Pranjal does not need words to tell him that she absolutely loves what she sees. The mantra to a good start in a relationship is being instinctively aware of the needs of your loved ones.

They are happy—deliciously, deliriously, happy. Life with Ruby far exceeds every kind of pleasure Pranjal has ever had earlier. He even starts giving their men's night out a miss. He refuses to waste any more time without her by his side. He always manages to come up with innovative temptations to entice her.

Bengali and Tamil cultures fascinate Ruby. Indian history, travelling to villages (that's where the unpretentious people live, she declares) across the country, Punjabi food, interacting with new people, Sufi music, Salsa dancing and listening to Pranjal recite romantic poetry over a glass of wine in their balcony make her happy.

It is Tagore and Keats they indulge in when their mood is mellow. The Romantic poets of course stressed emotion over reason. Keats elevated it to another dimension by giving himself so totally up to the cult of sensuous beauty. In his present state of mind, Pranjal can bond with the great poet's disinclination to elaborate upon a complete moral or social philosophy in his poetry.

He ceases to mull over Kafka's anti-fairy tale questions. Unlike the master storyteller's characters, Pranjal is not an alienated individual in this modern world. Love has elevated him to a stratum where ecstasy dwells. This euphoric state of his mind, receptive only to immediate sensation, is appositely mirrored in his poetry, which is no longer a realm of the sweet pining thoughts of melancholy. Rather, Pranjal's verses are now the ardent songs of fulfilment.

Cynicism, criticism and all other pessimistic emotions somehow melt away like the burnt-out wax of a candle leaving behind only love, radiant as the brilliant illumination. The lightness in their happy hearts effectively establishes the superficiality of gloominess.

'Pranjal these days writes love songs instead of serious poetry.' Anita drawls mockingly to her colleagues at the office. 'Imagine the plight of good literature if our writers and poets started regressing to the world of ideological impracticality of an immature mind instead of practically progressing with the times.'

'The focus and stance of the poet is an individual perspective.' Pranjal replies tersely.

'One's outlook should mature with age,' Anita mocks.

'Being mature does not necessitate being jaded. One can continue to embrace the enthusiasm of youth throughout one's lifetime to enjoy endless happiness,' Pranjal replies.

'I can't believe this, my dear Pranjal is now philosophising!' Anita exclaims dramatically.

Pranjal courteously excuses himself out of the room.

At home, Pranjal forgets about his confrontation with Anita at the office. Happiness lifts his spirits as soon as Ruby opens the door to their home. Ruby has enhanced Pranjal's responsiveness to his surroundings. Delhi is no longer simply the sprawling capital of the country where the cacophony of impatient drivers and extreme indifference towards civic etiquette rule.

Delhi has wide avenues lined with luxuriantly green margosa trees. The young neem leaves are shining green and artistically tinted with rust. The streets are not crowded but teeming with interesting people. The markets are not congested but vibrant with life. Ruby has a positive vibrator fitted firmly on her mind so that she spends minimum energy fretting over issues beyond her control.

Delhi being the ultimate destination of all those who relish the power game of politics in the country, the area around Vijay Chowk—particularly the Sansad Bhawan building, where the election winners are sworn in—is the coveted region among the politicians.

Pranjal has driven past Raisina Hill—the mound on which the Rashtrapati Bhawan, the President's House, stands—countless number of times admiring the flaming orange sunset behind the imposing domes, pillars and columns designed by Sir Edwin Landseer Lutyens. Sitting on the lawns of the India Gate, he has even penned a few poems admiring the magnificent legacy the British left behind.

However, it is Ruby who brilliantly brings alive the regal atmosphere that prevailed around the avenue during the British Raj, with her vast knowledge of history. Ruby draws a richly engaging pen picture of the scenery that existed, and effectively ignites an intense craving within her reader to go back in time to experience the grandeur that existed.

Then she bluntly points out that the exquisite wonder of the present-day democracy is that it allows even ordinary folks like them to drive right up to the President's gates. Just like that. In fact, they even visit the Mughal Gardens within the President's estate during spring, when the doors are open to the public to feast their eyes in the colourful panorama. The garden, a work of art by Sir Lutyens for Lady Harding, combines formal Mughal style with British garden designs.

Ruby's encyclopaedic knowledge on almost every topic and her aptitude to assess the facts in the present context never ceases to amaze Pranjal.

Pranjal treated knowledge as a tool to barter money. Additional qualification meant better placements. Pranjal always studied with the objective of acquiring a better position. He is flummoxed watching Ruby gather knowledge with no definite purpose but purely for the pleasure of knowing.

On his way to work, Pranjal drives by an ancient-looking peepal tree everyday. Apart from an appreciative cursory glance at it sometime, he has never paid attention to the tree.

'No wonder the Buddha attained enlightenment meditating under a peepal tree.' Ruby mouthed the words as they crossed the tree while driving down to Delhi to watch a play.

'Pardon?' Pranjal asks. She does catch him unawares.

'There was a time in India when the peepal tree was revered as the *tree of life*. The remarkable feature of this tree is that its branches morph into roots. Thus, it grows both upwards and downwards. So even when the original tree decays and perishes, its branches underneath remain young and continue to enclose the parent.'

'The Great Banyan tree in the Kolkata botanical garden is said to be over 250 years old with 2800 prop roots covering an area of 1.5 hectares. Both the banyan and the peepal belong to genus *Ficus*.' Ruby can impart random *gyan* (knowledge) on any subject.

'I've admired the old peepal tree many times while driving past. However, I have never looked up any information on the tree,' Pranjal says.

'Good boy! So you do notice the beauty of nature when not concentrating on the PYTs around!'

'Very funny.' He does not tell her she is the only pretty, young thing his eyes ever focus on ever since she sauntered into his life.

It does not distress Ruby that the fruit seller fleeces her by quoting a higher price when she steps out to purchase fruits, when the boys leer at her when she walks down to a store, or when women stare at her like they would an exotic flamingo strolling alongside the representatives of beauty of the womenfolk.

Nothing bad can put Ruby down, for her good things lie in very strange places. She explains the fruit seller's cheating attitude as his survival instinct to carry on with the business of living in an unjust world by making a quick buck through unfair means.

At least the bugger is engaged in a legal occupation, she reasons. He could well cross over to the other side of the law to make ends meet, adding another number to the increasing populace of criminals. It is far safer to have him preoccupied with petty cheating than have him end up a criminal.

Those youngsters are just not worth worrying over as long as they do not encroach upon one's physical space. Until they learn to be responsible in a socially mature culture and until the time when they have ample work and entertainment to lead a fruitful life, it is pointless being hassled over a state of affairs that is beyond one's control.

As for the critically scrutinizing women, where has gossip ever taken a backseat? What is more, if one happened to be the topic of conversation due to one's strangeness, so be it. They were welcome to devote their precious time discussing her. However, she refused to squander away her valuable energy thinking about those who talked about her needlessly.

'When I refuse to acknowledge their presence, their negative actions automatically get relegated to the recess of my memory and perforce fade away from me and I manage to conserve my energy for better things. As long as I can steer my thoughts to remain pure, I am able to wish them away from touching my life,' Ruby maintains.

Ruby unwaveringly views adversity from a positive perspective, which gives her a broader vision and ample space to nurture hope for a brighter future. Her eternal hope transcends her into a state of bliss.

'Why can't I focus on scaling down the magnitude of my problems? Why is my life such a complex, knotted contraption?' Pranjal ponders, fervently wishing he could free himself from the countless chains that drag his pace and prevent him from living blissfully.

'And it is not as if highly qualified women do not stoop down to pander to their baser instincts by playing sophisticated games of jealousy. Last week, my friend Kavya and I attended a book reading; the book was written by Mrs Rahman, who is an award-winning writer and a senior professor from one of the leading universities. After the function, we sat drinking tea together with two reviewers present there as we had ample time on our hands. Kavya started reading one of my stories aloud for want of anything better to do. One of the critics, Dr Mamta, who was drinking tea with us, thinking Mrs Rahman had written the piece, waxed eloquence on the text, style and content of the story. When Kavya introduced me as the writer, the literary reviewer fell silent.'

'Planned denial has remained a classy and effective technique of rejection in our society.' Ruby smiles wearily. 'The only difference in my approach is that I reverse my focus and concentrate on the rejection of the negative attributes as opposed to the rejection of the positive traits of an individual.'

Pranjal observes that she also makes subtle changes to slip into the cloak of this intriguing multicultural city. She does not venture to the vegetable market in her stretch jeans that so lovingly hugs her curves. She rarely ventures out in skirts anymore. To make herself inconspicuous, she has several sets of *salwar* suits switched in all hues of the colour of darkness. She happily believes that she now pretty much blends into the scenery. After all, for the majority of the officers' wives, the dress code for casuals is the *salwar* suit.

To Pranjal, Gurgaon now appears so much more than merely a swanky part of the NCR (National Capital Region), where one had relocated for a better pay package.

He had moved to new Gurgaon, a rapidly developing, most happening city in the country, instead of travelling overseas. There was no lure for him to shift base to foreign shores. His migration would not elevate his family prestige. He did not need to escape any traditional caste hierarchies either. He wished to remain close to home. Close to Ma.

'According to the epic tale Mahabharata, prince Yudhishthir presented Gurgaon, earlier termed *Gurugram, as guru dakshina* to the spiritual leader Dronacharya,' Ruby says.

'Haryana is not merely a state where female infanticide was once rampant… Ruby reminds Pranjal, '…it is in Haryana, the land of immense riches—*bahudhana* and plentiful grain *bahudhanya*—that the great sage Ved Vyas is said to have written what is probably the longest poem in the world, the Mahabharata.'

'Well, being a poet of this modern age, I guess I was destined to wander into the land famous for its legendary poem.' Pranjal grins.

'Haryana is the land where the well-loved Hindu Lord Krishna preached the Bhagavadgita at the start of the battle of Mahabharata. The profound philosophy advocated by the Bhagavadgita, of the supremacy of duty, has become the foundation of Indian culture. You know, Lord Krishna is said to have dwelled in Braj, which includes districts of Haryana, Uttar Pradesh and Rajasthan. Braj is not a region on the map but it was the abode of Krishna on earth. Krishna was born in Mathura. In the woods of Vrindavan he frolicked with the young *gopis*, cow-herd girls, and wooed Radha.'

Ruby further enlightened him that *vrinda* refers to Goddess Tulsi and *Vrindavan* was thus named because *tulsi* (basil) plants grew profusely in the forest. Tulsi plants are venerated and worshipped in Hindu households.

Ruby's flair in seamlessly unfolding the past to enhance the beauty of the present lends a captivatingly harmonizing effect to a place. Imagining an enticing past somehow augments the beauty of a place presently suffocated with the burden of humanity.

Ruby's only grudge against Gurgaon is the lack of pedestrian facilities. Like Ma, she scoffs at driving when the distance allows for walking.

Unfortunately, India's millennium city, Gurgaon, unlike other metropolitan cities in so many different parts of the world, does not encourage its inhabitants to walk. There are barely any pedestrian paths. Trees sprout out in stretches where narrow footpaths are constructed and electric poles shoot up obstructively in the track and effectively discourage walking. Tragically, where the pavement is wide, many homeless quickly occupy the area as a permanent settlement by setting up all their cooking utensils and assorted rags for a comfortable living.

Ruby is not discouraged though; like so many young people in this country of extreme disparity, she writes stories on the lives of these people, optimistic of creating public awareness, of change. As she trudges determinedly through the dusty streets, her car lies forlornly in the basement parking.

For Ruby, every little event is an occasion of celebrating life. Every day is a new learning experience. This is perhaps why life with her is always so refreshingly youthful. Ruby's presence in Pranjal's life has totally transformed his perspective of living. He no longer is content with his routine existence. He wants to spend every moment he can with her and relish life in all its magnificent magnitude.

Pranjal's life has changed from that of a routine exhausting office existence with a Friday night party with his friends at their weekend watering hole to dust off some of their general fatigue, to one of fun and excitement.

The tavern with its rustic ambience is a drunkard's paradise. The customers purchase the booze from the wine shop outside and carry it along with them. The waiters serve chicken *tikka* or paneer *tikka* in Salem stainless steel plates and bring along complimentary flimsy plastic glasses for the drinks. The food served—elastic *naans* and greasy *biryani*—is tasteless. However, the alcohol effectively does the work of anaesthetizing their taste buds as they gratify their rumbling stomachs.

'Rajvir, check that chick out in the red shirt. What human ingenuity man! A woman squeezes into a shirt half of her size and still the material does not rib apart! Man, get a look at her.' Rajeev is generally the first to get drunk. Two straight shots and he begins rambling.

'*Arre bhai,* Rajeev, two drinks and you are drunk. You are a townie. A decade with Rajpal and me and you're still a wimp,' Rajvir despairs.

Rajpal and Rajvir nonchalantly consume by the litre, whereas Rajvir turns introspective after several pegs, Rajpal remains in control. The infallible sense of reliability his persona emanates remains stable.

'She reminds me of a sausage,' Pranjal comments.

'A sausage. That's a good one. A florescent pink sausage. Ha, ha.' With two pegs, Rajeev's sense of humour flowers full bloom.

Book launches, theatre, cultural nites, high-profile dinners, village weddings, exotic Japanese meals in fine restaurants and street food at the local *dhaba*—with Ruby there is an Aladdin's treasure in every nook and corner of Delhi and Gurgaon.

Pranjal feels his cup of contentment surely is overflowing. Weekdays, he returns home to Ruby with the impatience of a teenager in love. They go out almost every evening, for drives, dinners or to spend a couple of hours with old friends, relations and new acquaintances.

Pranjal finds himself distancing from his close friends Rajpal, Rajvir and Rajeev. It is not that he desires their company less; it is simply that he has to meet them alone as they do not consider it appropriate for their families to accompany them when they visit. Pranjal feels that maintaining a relation with friends after marriage where social interaction with the family is avoided is a rather strenuous matter.

Rajpal is very particular about his wife not interacting with women from outside their village. The only time Pranjal has seen his wife was during their marriage, which was years back. Rajvir firmly believes a woman's place is at home. Family outings are restricted to visiting relatives. Rajeev resides alone in Gurgaon. His wife lives with their two sons with his parents in his native place. He wishes to bring up his children in a stable atmosphere, undisturbed by the harassments of his transfers.

Earlier the friends frequented local bars, drinking into the night as they pondered over investments in shares and property and discussed women.

Rajvir is thirty-five, deceptively lean and packs a mean punch. With his casual gait, a relaxed demeanour, he appears to be content watching life from the sideline. It does not take one long to discover that underneath the nonchalant stance is an intelligent brain strategizing innovative ways to multiply money.

Rajvir has a knack of fishing out profit-making shares. All four men benefit from his insight. He comes from a family of landowners and property dealers. He has become a multibillionaire from a humble-salaried supervisor in a medium-size private company, after the property boom escalated in Gurgaon. All his ancestral property that had supported the family with a comfortable life with rich harvests of wheat and paddy suddenly sprouted gold as land prices skyrocketed.

Rajpal's is a similar story of becoming a billionaire overnight by selling land. However, Rajpal is passionately involved with his job. He enjoys its adventure and excitement and the fame it has given him in his village.

Rajeev is the handsome one among the four friends. He has a way with the girls. With his extraordinary good looks and beguiling charm, he never needed to try too hard to get a partner to dance with when they painted the town red during their weekends' pub-hopping marathons. Although, technically, Pranjal was the only bachelor among the four, he never felt that he was in the company of married men.

Rajeev and Rajvir rarely behaved as if they had wives at home. While Rajvir was extremely discreet about his women, Rajeev openly flaunted his relationships. Observing Rajeev conduct his long-distance marriage in such a farcical manner, Pranjal wondered precisely what purpose did a marriage serve.

'What about your wife?' Pranjal asks Rajeev. The latter announces his plans to take off on a weekend trip with his passion of the season to Thailand.

'What about her?' Rajeev looks at him with the innocence of a five year old.

'Well, she'll be waiting for you back home. I mean you two are committed to one another in a marriage, aren't you?' Pranjal fumbled. Marriages all around him made little sense to him. Such insensitive attitude of his father towards his mother had angered him when he was a young boy.

'Grow up, Pranjal. My wife stays at home. I am a very responsible husband. I send her a fat cheque every month and visit her whenever I am free. But a man needs some fun *yaar*. And wives are not meant to serve that purpose.' Rajeev smoothly explains his action.

'Yeah. But what's the harm in having fun with your wife? You could all go on a family holiday. She would enjoy it. So would the children.'

'Yeah. She would enjoy it. The kids would enjoy it. But man, what about me? I've worked like a dog the entire month. I need to unwind. I can't do that with the responsibility of the wife and kids dangling around my neck,' Rajeev exclaims.

Pranjal opens his mouth to advise Rajeev against thus hurting his wife, but closes it just as swiftly before articulating his thoughts for that black shroud nagging his peace of mind threatens to bounce forth centre stage.

Ever since his marriage, however, he finds that he can no longer work up a desire to seek entertainment without Ruby. No matter how unfashionable it sounds, she is the embodiment of all the pleasure he ever desired.

Perhaps, had his friends included their wives in their outings, they would have continued to socialize. Stag parties now appear a waste of valuable time to him.

Pranjal prefers hanging around their apartment in his pyjamas, reading poetry or some old classic from Ruby's voluminous collection of books during weekends. Dressing to go out for Sunday lunch appears an unnecessary effort. And the company of his three male friends seems a trifle too bland.

Ruby and Pranjal generally experiment with new cuisines every weekend for lunch. Weekends are for relaxing nowadays. He no longer feels that old urge to get ready as soon as he wakes up at around noon to go to the café across the street for a strong cup of coffee and a bite to eat before lunch, which he invariably had with his friends at their regular *dhaba*. His friends preferred eating out, as cooking non-vegetarian meals is taboo in their home kitchens. What is more, they all indulged in non-vegetarian food, even during the scorching dry north Indian summers.

Pranjal invites his friends for dinner a couple of times to treat them with Ruby's scrumptious cooking. Unfortunately, they come sans their wives even when he specifically requests them to bring along their spouses. So Ruby plays the perfect hostess and serves dinner and graciously retreats after serving the food, sensing how stilted the conversation becomes during her presence.

Pranjal begins to resent his friends for not making an effort to include her in their conversations. After all, she is an interesting and intelligent woman. Nevertheless, the lull in their conversation ebb only when she excuses herself from the room, thus changing well-laid arrangements of family dinners into those of bachelor parties.

Instead of wasting time hanging out with the men every evening, Pranjal meets them for a drink and a round of billiards at the club every Sunday evening these days. If he could have had it his way, he would have avoided the weekend pool game as well. However, Ruby insists that he meet them at least once a week. Otherwise, they will accuse her of stealing their friend away from them she comments in jest.

'How can they accuse you when I am the one reluctant to remain separated from you even for a moment?' Pranjal asks. Ruby, remarks that someday they could also avoid him when he needed their company.

The truth is Pranjal has outgrown his carefree days. However, drowning scotch, brainstorming over property rates and the share market still hold his interest.

His friends are far better off financially. Yet, Pranjal finds that their thirst for acquisition of wealth remains as unquenchable as his. It is almost as if they are addicted to their wealth. Rajvir is tight-fisted with his money. Although he is undoubtedly the richest among them, he is also always the last one to offer to pay a bill. Rajvir has four houses, five cars and three children. He spends generously on his children, giving them the best education and dressing them up in the most expensive branded outfits available in the big city malls.

Spending so much time in their company, Pranjal has learnt to multiply his assets. Further, he has become a trite too thrifty.

'This obsession to constantly make more money is also a *nasha*, Pranjal.' Rajpal says nursing his drink as they sit in their regular *dhaba*. 'Unless we learn to get a grip on our greed, the lure of money will coil around one's being like a slimy serpent.'

'We are not committing any irregularities here. The builder is going to mint money. We are only asking him to pay us a small percentage for introducing him to the buyers,' Pranjal replies.

'There's always a very thin line that separates the right from the wrong, the legal from the illegal, the truth from the untruth. Tread carefully, friend. You'll be passing on your values to the next generation.'

'First, one needs a firm foundation of money. Values will follow. In this world, money power and status talk far more loudly than values, Rajpal,' Pranjal says.

'You also need a *maksat*—a vision in life, brother…' Rajpal's booming voice lends a strange contrast to mouthing his homilies, '…a vision to lead a meaningful life. You know what—I have no fear of dying with my boots on as long as I am able to continue to clean out as many vermin from this world.'

'It's easy for you to talk about high ideals, Rajpal. You have enough cash stacked up, so you need not worry about your and your children's future.'

'That may be so. But it is my work and the sense of fulfilment I experience performing my duty that gives a meaning to my existence. The joy of commitment to one's purpose in life. That is the legacy I wish to leave behind for my children. We cannot always hoard our money close to our heart, Pranjal. But the elemental sense of contentment we experience on having performed well in our chosen path is a sublime feeling that we can clutch within us forever.' Rajpal's over six feet bulky frame hid a heart of gold as quietly and distinctly as the touch of smile that lingered on his moustached face to expose a fleeting glimpse of vulnerability in his towering personality.

Chapter 6

Ruby has engaged a house cleaner, named Dhani. Dhani lives in a rented accommodation in the neighbouring village. Her work hours are from nine to five. Although there is not much work in the house with just two people in there, Ruby reasons that even if for nothing else, but to answer the door, they need someone around the house during her working hours.

Ruby pays Dhani a very handsome salary with annual increments, weekly offs, festival leave and a bumper one-month annual vacation for the family to go to their native village. Dhani is apparently devoted to her. After all, her whole life changed from one of hapless despair to that of a happy and comfortable one—all thanks to Ruby's generosity.

'Must you give her so many off days?' Pranjal asks as he watches Ruby vacuum clean the house.

'She is a human being as well. If we so-called educated ones don't show them the path to be humane, who will?'

'I just hope she realizes how lucky she is to have an employer like you.'

'As long as I am doing my duty, my conscience is clear. I won't wish to leave behind this world knowing I had knowingly committed a wrong to anyone,' Ruby says. 'Dhani now looks tidy, dresses neatly and maintains cleanliness. Yesterday, Mrs Sinha asked her to work for her. Can you imagine it is the same person against whom Dhani was complaining for calling her a low caste. Still, it's wonderful to see that caste prejudices cease to exist once your work starts to speak for you.'

'I remember Dhani crying on your lap the day Mrs Sinha derided her as a low born. That was the day you gave her one of your saris to comfort her,' Pranjal says.

'Dhani came this morning to tell me that Mrs Sinha has asked her to work for her after she completes her work here,' Ruby says.

'I thought Dhani is a full-time help. Aren't you paying her the salary of a fulltime, and then some more?' Pranjal enquires.

'I am. I have told her that if she is dissatisfied she must give up her work here. Imagine she takes leave every other day owing to her own ill health or the sickness of her family members. Where does she have the extra time for additional work? She barely has the energy to complete the work we have employed her to do,' Ruby says.

For Ruby, charity is an essential part of existence, even if it means doing half the house cleaner's work herself.

So far, Pranjal had accumulated affluence for a comfortable future, wrote poetry and played guitar to gratify his creative urges, worked at a reputable company to lead a routine life and keep Ma happy.

Ruby's harmonious conduct seeps into the atmosphere to sway Pranjal to align his actions to the ministering of his inner voice. Pranjal increasingly finds himself seeking a purpose-driven life in which he is no longer drifting aimlessly in his journey. He sets out to chisel all his flaws and strive towards his goal of becoming a progressive human being. He can foresee himself moving in the direction of a major transformation in his attitude towards his life.

Pranjal realizes that he is dangerously close to falling in love with Ruby. He had never been in love before, never loved the women he had dated before meeting Ruby. The few girls he knew now compare no better than faded black-and-white photographs to Ruby's vivacious presence, which somehow turned his world to a multicoloured extravaganza.

Ruby has magically transformed their barren terrace into a veritable jade forest garden of Assam.

Seasonal flowers burst colourfully into bloom with every change of season. A bright mass of dazzling white African daisies herald the spring. The nodding clerodendron or the bridal veil with its pendulous white flowers held in loose panicles cascade down like a shower of fragrance.

The elegantly white Amazon lily enhances the sweet scent of the garden, as do the pinwheel-shaped, snow-white angel wing jasmine and the Azores jasmine. Pansies, asters, flox, petunias… splash colour to rejuvenate the spirit. With carpet grass covering every inch of the area in the terrace, it is easy for Pranjal to forget that they are not in fact, living in the ground floor.

Bougainvilleas bloom in a multitude of different colours the year round providing a tranquil escape as the branches creep along the intricately woven cane supports Ruby has strategically set up to cunningly manoeuvre the pattern of their growth. Lured by such sylvan surroundings, Pranjal finds that his day is incomplete without sitting in this paradise every evening. The aroma, colour and the sylvan surroundings have a positive therapeutic power to still even his worst mood swings.

He needs to calm his disposition ever so often these days. The other evening, he had taken Ruby to the wedding of the daughter of a senior executive, Mr Goel. Wedding planners and caterers very professionally managed the nuptials.

However, keeping in tune the present-day commercialization, even though no expense had been spared to arrange for a grand wedding, there was no evidence of a personal touch to such a cherished affair as a marriage. There was loud DJ music with a dance floor where children and several couples gyrated. The bride and the groom sat on a decorated platform in their finery.

Practical guests arrived with small envelopes and handed them over to Mr Goel. Everyone gave an envelope to him and headed for the food lined up all around the pavilion—*shamiana*. They piled their plates with food and ate their full. After all, they had paid for dinner in those envelopes. *Paisa vasool.*

Ruby and Pranjal made the effort to pick up a beautiful ethnic tea set for the newly weds from the Indian Emporia. They had even had it tastefully wrapped in handmade paper. This was the first wedding reception they were attending as a couple.

Unfortunately, at the function, they are the only ones who arrive with a gift. There is no practice of wishing the newly wed and presenting them with a present as a token of affection. Pranjal and Ruby are conspicuous with their colourfully wrapped souvenir, which stands out like a sore big toe in the delicate feet of a princess.

'Good evening sir, Congratulations!' Pranjal says. 'This is my wife.' Mr Goel hurriedly grabs the gift without so much as acknowledging Ruby's presence.

Pranjal sulks morosely having suffered Mr Goel's affront. He watches him fuss over the VIPs and promises not to attend another colleague's family wedding until he has reached a senior most privileged position.

He is miffed at being ignored, conveniently forgetting that he has not reached the enviable position of power wherein an effort would be made especially to greet him, a smile stretched to welcome him, an arm extended forward to usher him into a gathering.

'Hey, I made some hot chocolate,' Ruby grins. She sets the tray with the cups on the cane table and sits down on the cane sofa beside him, snuggling up into him like a little puppy.

'What were you thinking?' Ruby asks. 'You had an awful expression in your face just now.'

'Last night. It was horrible. I am sorry you had to suffer humiliation because of me. We shouldn't have attended the wedding reception,' Pranjal says. 'A standard response I would have expected would be of him to greet you, introduce us to the newly weds and insist that we do not leave without eating a morsel at least. This minimum courtesy takes barely a minute. The guests sometimes travel hours braving the notorious traffic in an effort to attend a wedding. The bloke did not even have the minimum decency to offer a smile. And it isn't as if there were so many guests. His much-hyped big fat wedding had no soul for me.'

'It wasn't your fault. I think we have to update ourselves with the scenario here,' Ruby says. 'Number one, people here do not appreciate gifts. So next time we attend such a function, remember, no gifts. We will just fill an envelope like everybody else.

'Look at the amount Mr Goel had to spend on the wedding. And he is your colleague, earning as much as you do from the office as salary. He has no inheritance, no other member of his family is earning. Imagine the burden it must be on him to arrange such a lavish wedding. I mean they must have spent a lifetimes' savings on their daughter's marriage. I suppose the idea of gifting money is to help the bride's father a bit. Beautiful presents, which the newly wed may never use, have less value compared to hard cash that comes handy at such times,' Ruby says.

'You always remember with fondness Phukan Aunty every time you use the crystal salad bowl she gifted, Saikia Aunty every time you lovingly spread the tablecloth she embroidered on the dining table, Das Aunty and Dutta Aunty every time you use the rice cookers they gifted. These gifts have entered our household as reminders of their affection and blessing,' Pranjal observes.

'Perhaps so. But to give suitable gifts one needs to be in tune with what the couple will need the most. This is possible only if the families are in close contact.' Ruby says. 'However, due to the immensely competitive lifestyle here, there is little effort to maintain humane relationships. There is hardly any time to lead a relaxed and happy life.'

'You have to admit that life is invariably a little more relaxed when there is old wealth to fall back on,' Pranjal says.

'Alternatively, one could also teach oneself to exercise self-restraint and learn to be happy with a little less.'

'My dear, the concept you are advocating goes against the underlining code of conduct of our rapidly striding consumerist society,' Pranjal says.

'Well, life is motion. I fully agree that without the dynamics of business, there can be no progress. However, balance is the key to a happy life.'

'It is easy to advocate about maintaining a balance. But when one is from the bottom of the social ladder, the eternal aspiration to step up rapidly as many steps as possible remains the driving force of one's existence,' Pranjal reiterates.

'An extremely dangerous situation to be in psychologically. Healthy competition and ambition is good. But becoming robotic in search of material nirvana is no more than a pipe dream,' Ruby states.

'You have to experience what it feels like to become invisible in society to truly appreciate one's eternal hunger to aspire for power and status,' Pranjal says.

'Society cannot make us invisible when we are focused on discharging our duties religiously. It can only make us invisible when we allow the dictates of social hierarchy; be it caste, community, status—whatever to dominate us.'

'Easier said than done my dear philosopher wife,' Pranjal replied to Ruby.

'You will learn. Life will teach you its philosophy through its practicality,' Ruby pauses before continuing. 'Now to get to rule number two while attending an urban wedding. Remember, guests do not expect the hosts to urge them to partake of the food, buffet here means not only self-service but also self-invite. Since we are not comfortable with eating in other people's parties sans a cordial offering, we need not eat. Nothing to fuss about.

'Rule number three: since most of these invitations are from people you interact with in your official capacity, your attending such receptions alone is more than adequate. My accompanying you is superfluous and unnecessary. Therefore, I am given the royal ignore.

'I have enough confidence in me to grasp that I am not overlooked because I am insignificant or because I am a failure. It is merely a question of my being not relevant to these people.

'Straightforward and uncomplicated! We cannot change what we do not like, but that does not mean that we remain aloof from the society in which we need to survive. Simply slip into their mode for those moments. Life then becomes less complicated for everybody.'

Ruby swiftly assessed the value system of the society she had interacted with ever so briefly. Without hesitation, she voiced her feelings to her husband.

In this serene space, Pranjal and Ruby are able to communicate their thoughts without restraint. The beautiful garden is surely a good augur of their bright future.

Chapter 7

'Wake up! Come on Pranjal. Wake Up!' Ruby has a cup of tea ready for Pranjal.

'It's Saturday. It is a holiday. We should be sleeping late,' Pranjal complains. 'Anyway, it's still dark outside.'

'Not today, we aren't lazybones. We are going to watch a beautiful sunrise together. Let's drive down to Sultanpur.'

'Sultanpur bird sanctuary? We never made any such plans!' Pranjal exclaims.

'Why do we need to always make prior plans? Let's just take off.'

'I don't do that. I mean we can't just take off without proper plans.'

'Of course we can. We are both free this weekend. Come on.'

Sultanpur is just fifteen kilometers away from Gurgaon and is a good winter weekend gateway. Ruby is as avid an avian watcher as Pranjal. As the delicate light of dawn surfaces into the darkness of the night, Pranjal finds himself perched on a vantage position to get a ringside view of the winged wonders.

'Early morning is the time when their activity is greatest. They are likely to sing their sweetest songs loud and clear during the virgin hours.' Ruby whispers softly in the silence of nature.

Red-wattled lapwings, herons, plovers, white ibises, cormorants, painted storks and spoonbills inhabit this green glade. The grey-legged goose, shoveller and coot come through China during the winters. Winter is the time that heralds the winged visitors from as far off as Siberia.

Ruby and Pranjal ramble around the sanctuary, searching for feathers those beautiful birds might have shed, yelping and jumping like their primitive ancestors on finding a plume, fondly collecting their treasure in a large paper bag to take them home as souvenirs of a wonderful weekend.

They spend the day in their room. Talk the night away sitting beneath the streaming willow trees, tucking in a very basic dinner of *roti* and *subzi*, sipping vintage red wine. In such idyllic environs, every morsel tastes like ambrosia.

'It's quite amazing. I'm actually enjoying this whole nature trip.' Pranjal remarks bemused at the discovery, the wine gently relaxing him.

'See, you're not such a big city guy at heart after all,' Ruby grins widely exposing her pearly whites.

'You're changing me, woman. You are changing me,' Pranjal says.

'It is not me. It's you. You are rediscovering the person you are… the person you buried deep within you in your aggressive pursuit of materialism.'

'Isn't it a tad too ideological to be against money, which has the power to buy us so much? And that includes our basic needs, comfort and security,' Pranjal asks.

'I would be a fool to say that money should not be courted at all. What I am saying is that we should be mindful of appreciating money as a tool instrumental in providing us with the comforts we desire. We don't need to become addicted to its powerful potency and become enslaved by it.'

'I am caught in the whirlpool of the high one experiences at one's power to accumulate money, I guess.' Pranjal reluctantly admits after a long moment of contemplation.

'It's in everyone's mind these days. This competitive urge to make more money, live an even better life. Ruby, money buys not merely material things but respect in society as well,' Pranjal says.

'Absolutely. In fact, we would not even be enjoying this moment in nature if we did not have the money at our disposal. What I am saying is we should be weary of not selling our souls simply to savour all that we desire. By disciplining ourselves, we can empower our mind to enjoy what we can afford without constantly salivating for more. I understand hunger is the motivation that fires ambition, which is so essential for the dynamic progress of society.' Ruby pauses and reiterates. 'However, my firm belief is that to maintain a balanced outlook is an absolute necessity for a good life.'

Ruby is a travel writer. She contributes articles to several major international magazines and writes a fortnightly column on lifestyle issues. She needs to travel around to collect matter for her writing. Pranjal starts trying to fit his schedule around her travels so that they can enjoy discovering new places together.

Travelling for Pranjal so far had meant executive class tour, staying in the best hotels and using the services of a chauffer-driven car to look up the sights. With Ruby, he learns to expect the unexpected. There are times she pleasantly surprises him by accompanying in his tours and remaining holed up in their hotel suite the whole day watching television while he attends meetings. Afterwards, they explore the unusual sights of the area and always discover something interesting. Even if they find nothing terribly exciting in a particular destination, Ruby manages to unearth some fascinating detail and vastly enhance the importance of their visit.

Pranjal and Ruby mutually decided to skip a formal honeymoon, agreeing the idea is alien enough for them to make them feel uncomfortable. Pranjal's cousins mock him over their decision, ridiculing him of being stuck up. The important point is that Ruby and Pranjal are both happy with their decision. They emphatically establish that they do not need a formal period for romance. They would enjoy a romantic life together instead. They promised one another.

'I've taken up a project on writing a series of articles on Haryana.' Ruby announces grandly, barely a year into their marriage.

'Eh? But I thought you weren't planning to take up any work for a whole year.' Pranjal does not want her to work. He wants her to be free to spend time with him without being bound to set a schedule.

'It's January. We celebrated our first anniversary last month, remember?' Ruby says.

They did invite a few friends and acquaintances to their garden party at home. Ruby lit earthen lamps and placed them strategically around their garden. The effect was ethereal. The night was fragranced by a sweet breeze perfumed with the profusion of the blossoming *champa*, jasmine and *sewali* flowers. There was the seductive sound of water sinuously flowing down the terracotta fountains laden with colourful stones—forest green, midnight-black, pure-white and rose-hued.

The arrangements were faultless that evening. The food was delectable. The weather was ideal. The guests had a great time, if only it had not been Anita out to create mischief. They invited her because Ruby insisted it would be an uncalled for affront to snub her. Yet, Anita spent the entire evening backbiting Ruby, maliciously ignoring her, refusing to acknowledge her as Pranjal's companion even when formally introduced.

'Pranjal, all my friends attend my Friday parties except you. So many of our college friends come—Neeraj, Atul and Kevin are regulars. It is a fun way to kickstart the weekend,' Anita said.

Looking at Anita is a similar experience to looking at a work of art. Her luscious honey-hued skin lends extra delicacy to her sensuously voluptuous figure. When she walks, not just her limbs move but her entire structure appears to glide in a sensual tale. It is only when she opens her mouth to articulate her thoughts that the disharmony in her vocal cords with the aesthetic perfection of her physical being stuns one out of the dream into the harsh discordant reality, very much reminiscent of an ice-cold bucket of water drenching one out of a reverie.

It is to her credit that she never faltered in her worship of Pranjal even when she had a long line of suitors vying for her attention.

'Neeraj and Kevin are partners. Atul is a bachelor. You delight in being the only woman in the party. So you obviously choose not to include Ruby in your invitation. Strange and archaic as it may sound to you, I enjoy socializing with Ruby. You will have to excuse us.' Pranjal tried to sound polite.

'Ruby and I.' Anita mimicked. 'God! You should hear yourself. Aren't you allowed to do anything by yourself? This crafty little wifey has you nicely wrapped in her little finger.'

'No. It is not her. It is me. I am bored of the monotonous singleton's lifestyle I was leading. I am comfortable this way.' Pranjal was irritated with her juvenile attempts at trying to undermine Ruby's character.

'Pranjal, you used to be such a party boy. You can't change your habits and tastes just because your wife doesn't share them,' Anita said.

'I have simply outgrown the wild teenage scene,' Pranjal said. 'Some people like to evolve with age, Anita.'

'She is too tame for you. I mean look at you and look at her. She is like a nun. A typical convent-educated properly disciplined old-fashioned British Memsahib, with no ambition whatsoever other than run the house in clockwork precision. Ugh! I bet the likes of her must be extinct species even in the remotest nook of the British Isles. And you, my dear, will soon tire of the novelty of her youth. For let's face it, Pranjal, it's that irresistible pull of youthful energy that has attracted you to her.' Academically, Anita is armed with a professional degree and is chronologically older than Ruby. Still she has no qualms about stooping down to manipulate and eliminate Ruby's presence from her path of victory.

'Sorry Anita, to deprive you of my company. Ruby's youthful energy is so encompassing that it has embraced me within its fold to rekindle within me the desire to experience life from a different perspective altogether. Ruby is a class apart. A gloriously sensual woman a man prays for but rarely gets. You know the difference between all the girls I have known and Ruby. In all the rest, what one sees is what one gets. With Ruby, what one sees is but merely a fraction of what one gets to discover. Do you honestly believe a guy like me would settle for anything less than his ideal woman?' Pranjal reacted brutally to Anita for voicing truths he wished to camouflage.

'I am the woman for you Pranjal. We are meant for one another. There can be no other woman for you. What I feel for you is real. You are too blind to realize it. We come from a similar background. We've both worked hard to reach where we are today. Miss Hoity, your dream princess, is the untouchable, proper elitist English-speaking Madam who has no idea what reality is all about. She lives in a dream world where everything is perfect. But you and I, we are creatures of the real world. We both have experienced how hard life can get. Dreams do not last a lifetime. Remember that Pranjal,' Anita stated.

Fortunately, Ruby announced dinner at that moment and saved the conversation from taking an ugly turn.

Pranjal remembers the celebration but conveniently forgets all about Ruby restarting her work. She does not need to work, he thinks resentfully. At the same time, he realizes that he cannot grudge her the satisfaction of gratifying her creative cravings.

Pranjal deliberately chooses to live outside the company premises. Instead of occupying an official quarter, he purchased an apartment close to the office. He is very particular about keeping his personal and professional life segregated. He avoids taking Ruby along to attend the official functions. He justifies his act by telling himself that there is no need to unnecessarily introduce her to all those women she will not be interested in meeting.

In truth, however, he knows she would enjoy an opportunity to interact with the women. After all, she specializes in writing human-interest stories. Being a freelancer, she is not part of a structured set up that facilitates a social network. Her social circle is restricted to mainly the editors she interacts with in her profession.

Pranjal realizes that Ruby misses the absence of a woman friend with whom she can communicate freely. However, if truth be told, it is because he wishes to maintain a safe distance between her and Anita that he has conscientiously refrained from introducing her to his colleagues. The havoc Anita created at the party is still chillingly fresh in his mind.

'Remove that petulant expression, Pranjal. I shall be mostly working from home except for some fieldwork. Moreover, fieldwork means more travel time for the two of us. I promise to adjust my travelling schedule to suit your work pressure.'

Pranjal is willing to allow her to cajole him like a six year old. 'Tell me about it.' He magnanimously invites her to elaborate.

'I have zeroed in on writing about the growth of Gurgaon, from a sleepy nondescript town to one of the best success stories in the country. I like this city. The vibrancy, the amazing skyline, the remarkable people.' Ruby shook her head in wonder. 'Do you realize it is one of the few cities in India where you will find people from across the country working and living? Perhaps it doesn't have enough recreation facilities for all its inhabitants, but it's got to be one of the better places to live in this country.'

'You like Gurgaon so much?' Pranjal wondered if she would not want to go back to Guwahati.

'Guwahati is home. We have our family there. Nonetheless, it is important to feel comfortable and respected in the city one is working in,' Ruby says. 'There is no question of ever severing links with our hometown and settling down in any other part of the country or world. I wish to spend the autumn of my life where I spent my youth,' she says.

'I agree. In the later years of our lives we will pine for the comfort of familiarity,' Pranjal says.

'Unless one has good friends, one will not be able to survive in this severely competitive metropolis,' Ruby says. 'Not after retirement, when people will refuse to even acknowledge one if one is a *persona non grata*.'

'True. Colleagues and acquaintances cannot be relied on for unconditional support.' Pranjal echoes words in tune with the rhythm of thoughts Ruby has expressed. He realizes that he has never seriously thought about the future and the place he would ultimately settle down in the later years of his life. The prospect of leisurely walking down the crowded streets of Guwahati to make a purchase and converse with the shopkeeper in Assamese does fill him with a warm sense of comfort and belonging.

'I don't wish to sound rigid in my outlook, but honestly, most acquaintances I have interacted here with so far appear way more familiar with the United States of America and England than they are to the part of the country we come from. Although we meet so many people from across the country settled or doing business in our region, for folks living here it is even more distant than the back of beyond.'

'True.' Pranjal agrees.

'On the other hand, most folks speak about the USA and parts of Europe almost as their second home. Strangely, our way of life is more unfamiliar to them than those of distant cultures. Although I have travelled to several countries, my knowledge of those overseas states is strictly limited to that of a mere temporary visitor. Their way of life, although enviable, is foreign to me. I guess I am much too comfortable with my space on earth to take the trouble to uproot my bearing and settle down in a world so different from my familiar surroundings,' Ruby says.

'It's strange that you should say that. You know, the reason I refused to move out of the country in search of better prospects is because I need to be close to home. Practically, everyone I knew accused me of taking a regressive step in refusing to move out,' Pranjal reflects. 'Even I had my doubts on my decision.

The occasional niggling thoughts of missed opportunities have raised their ugly head.'

'Doubts still persist?' Ruby enquires.

'Before I met you, I was still unsure whether my decision had been right. Then I look at you. You are so content with your space in this world that you do not even wish to relocate permanently to a different state, leave alone a different country. You are so obliviously unaffected by the constant sense of discontentment, which has become so fashionable these days. The unending hunger to get more out of every moment of life that was sucking me within its abyss has somehow, somewhere disappeared from my life,' Pranjal says.

'Being content does not make you a lesser person than the person who is always single-mindedly striding towards super success. Perhaps a little less fashionable. But never less intelligent,' Ruby says.

'Pundits overhearing our conversation are bound to despair and condemn us of being bigots who will doom the dynamics of civilization. But now that I think of it, we are fortunate to have the freedom to choose to stay home and not be burdened with the need to seek out greener pastures. Movement is inevitable when we are pursuing our education and are posted during our service life. But we are lucky to have the comfort of a home and family to return to, after retirement, should we so desire.'

'Yes, we should be grateful for our fortune,' Ruby says. 'More than anything else, this exposure here has further made me conscious of the fact that people of the various regions in our country are very different despite the common feeling of national affinity we share. I am learning so much about this vivid mosaic of cultures here everyday.'

Art, culture, literature fascinate Ruby. She has a collection of postcards of distant lands treasured in a pretty Kashmiri paper mache box that has a turquoise background and an orange floral pattern. In the restful evenings, they sit in their garden sipping hot chocolate and nibbling snacks. When they run out of interesting content to exchange, Pranjal randomly picks up a card and hands it over to Ruby. She transports him to the time and place of depiction in the picture by recounting the tale.

As a young boy, one of Pranjal's favourite heroes was Jason of Greek mythology. Jason looked like a golden god with the Golden Fleece in one of the postcards. When he read the story of Jason and the Golden Fleece, in the colourfully illustrated junior classic series, he dreamt of leading an adventurous life like Jason. When Ruby read about Jason by Apollonius of Rhodes in his epic poem Argonautica, Pranjal no longer aspired to follow Jason's footsteps. His treason to Medea, who had helped him claim the Golden Fleece by agreeing to marry Creusa, was not Pranjal's idea of how a hero ought to conduct his life.

'What kind of a hero would cheat on the woman who helped him win?' Ruby asks.

'The lowest scum.' Pranjal experiences a sharp physical pain in his chest. He ignores it, determined not to let his heart overpower his rational sense.

'But I have never thought of treachery. I would never leave Ruby after using her and then run away with Anita. Why am I feeling so guilty of an act of betrayal I have not even contemplated, let alone committed?' Such discomfiting thoughts trouble Pranjal's mind. 'But of course, you had ill intentions, Pranjal.' A voice within him mocks ruthlessly, refusing to be squashed under the might of his supreme indifference.

'Well, you can boast of being in the company of great thinkers who assumed a similar stance on Jason's conduct,' Ruby smiles and says. 'Even Dante in his 'Divine Comedy' (Canto XVIII), along with his guide, the Roman poet Virgil, watch as the devils whip and drives Jason to march the circle for eternity in Hell's Eight Circle (Bolgia 1).'

'What was it Anita had said about Ruby influencing my thoughts and beliefs?' Pranjal ponders. Although he had tried his best to shrug off Anita's shrewd observation, Pranjal is dismayed to discover that her remarks had sneakily penetrated within his intellect and sprouted their toxic tentacles, proliferating every nook and crevice therein. Pranjal finds himself wondering if indeed Ruby is out on a mission to alter his concepts. He wonders whether she is cleverly implanting her thoughts and beliefs into his mind, manipulating him to change into the person she wishes him to become.

From admiring the brash Jason, Pranjal begins to admire Dante Alighieri, the devout lover of Beatrice and the learner of divine things.

'No!' Pranjal reprimands himself. 'I am growing with Ruby, expanding my vision of life.'

'You need to maintain a distance in a relationship for it to flourish,' Anita had said.

As far as Ruby and Pranjal are concerned, they enjoy one another's company without feeling the need to maintain a so-called healthy distance; they even enjoy holidays together. Strangely, Pranjal never experienced an urge to get away from Ruby to unwind.

Chapter 8

'So tell me about your new project,' Pranjal now insists.

'I just learnt that ten years ago Gurgaon was nothing like this. In fact, it is only since the last five years that Gurgaon began its transformation. I often speak to Pavan, the boy who delivers our milk. His family owns six buffaloes and their farm, being adjacent to the main road, is now worth corers of rupees,' Ruby begins.

'You've been speaking to Pavan about his family?' Pranjal asks incredulously.

'How does anyone know anything about anybody without communicating? Do you realize this particular building we are living now stands in what were cultivated green fields a couple of years ago? That old neem tree over there...,' Ruby says, pointing to the tree scarcely ten yards away from their building.

'...That is the tree Pavan mentioned his grandfather and father used to rest under and eat their midday meals during the days when they cultivated these lands. And that peepal tree over there...' Ruby points to a tree almost thirty yards away from the neem tree.

'...Pavan's mother sat with her father one day when Pavan's father caught a glimpse of her under that tree. It is his good luck that his family choose the girl he had lost his heart on to become his wife. Here, marrying against the family wishes can result in dangerous consequences for the lovers.'

Pranjal silently marvels at the intricate workings of the feminine mind. When had Ruby drilled the young chap of such a treasure of family secrets? She hardly exchanged more than a few words with him while he poured the rich creamy milk from his sparkling clean stainless steel milk container into the saucepan.

'Pavan's mother is quite a looker and intelligent also!' Ruby smiles mischievously.

'Eh? How would you know?' Pranjal enquires.

'I visited their farm yesterday,' Ruby grins.

'You didn't?' Pranjal asks, perplexed at the idea of her roaming around unknown locality.

'Come on Pranjal. Don't get so worked up. They are nice folks. By the way, I chatted with Meera, that's Pavan's mother's name, for quite some time.' Ruby informs him.

'You did?' Pranjal is mystified.

'Pavan is her intelligent son. Ajay, her elder son, is not into academics. He looks after their buffaloes and helps around the house. Pavan is a bright student. He scored eighty percent in his tenth boards. He spends his day playing cricket. Full credit goes to Meera for bringing up such an obedient child. Imagine, he wakes up early in the morning and delivers our milk. A class eleven student!' Ruby exclaims.

'You are clearly impressed by Meera's disciplined upbringing of her sons,' Pranjal remarks.

'So would you be too if you could only grasp how alarming is the rate at which young boys are being spoiled here,' Ruby declares. 'Teenagers are drinking and embracing all the decadent habits due to the easy flow of money. Meera strictly avoids giving any money to her sons. She is illiterate but she has the sagacity of a highly educated woman. She has not given in to her son's demand for a car. She is very clear that her son will not drive a car until he has joined the IPS—Indian Police Service—or at least the Haryana State Police Service. The day he qualifies, she has promised to buy him the car of his choice.'

'Well, by then he would be able to buy his own car, won't he?' Pranjal grins.

'Here, have a look at this.' Ruby hands Pranjal a file, smartly ignoring his question. Pranjal gazes at the title, '*The Remains of Another Day....*'

Leafing through the pages, he is immersed in the engrossing yarn she has spun of a middle-aged couple exposed to a completely new civilization that springs right next door to their century-old ancestral home estate. While they continue to grow wheat and rear buffaloes, modern multistoreyed buildings mushroom almost overnight around them, flinging into their backyard a brand new lifestyle. The lush green fields of their neighbours now house aesthetically designed red-roofed white buildings for the urban dwellers who will be their new neighbours.

Who are the new neighbours with whom they will have the least interaction, who will ignore them and distance them from all social contact, who will never behave neighbourly towards them? Not during their lifetimes, at least. Neighbours, for whom their lifestyle will appear a curious oddity; the strange neighbours whose glances will linger at Meera's alluring voluptuous figure amply accentuated by her tight sweat-drenched braless blouse, her *lehanga* worn below her navel and her *chunni* covering her forehead; these neighbours, who will be instrumental in ushering in an unquestionable alteration to their social order.

'The green fields have disappeared,' Ruby wrote, 'altering a rural topography into an urban one. There is now tap water in Meera's house. This means she no longer needs to go to the village well to fill her pots. It also means that there is no longer a designated spot to exchange gossip daily. They have electricity in their house and a black-topped road right up to their farm. There are stores just outside the gate of her home, which sell grocery, making it unnecessary for Meera to make a monthly trip to the old village market. Meera is thrilled with these comfortable changes in her life.

'Most days when the setting sun, with its bold streaks of orange, colours the earth, Meera senses in her a heart-aching loneliness. She misses her immediate neighbour Rani and her family. In the days gone by, Rani and Meera would sit in the courtyard of either of their houses and converse in the evenings. Even during the daytime, they would meet and chop the vegetables together, chatting constantly.

'However, Rani and her family moved to a village almost four kilometres away after selling off their property for a tidy sum. They now meet occasionally.

'Meera does venture out to the new park when her friends from the nearby village urge her to accompany them, although she never really feels comfortable sitting in the park among the new dwellers. One or two women are friendly. But there are many who are rather toffee-nosed of their urban background.'

Ruby observes, 'I find this attitude of the city dwellers rather unsettling. To my mind, Meera is an intelligent and charming woman. She does not need the trimmings of a fancy city lifestyle to make her a better or a more interesting person. The adult education programme in the village school has armed her with the ability to read and write, and I was pleasantly surprised to hear from her that she enjoys reading. I gifted her a few books, which I purchased from the local market.

'Unlike many of the women living in the new buildings, there is not a pretentious bone in Meera's character. She speaks her mind freely. An acquaintance of mine who lives in our building scoffed at Meera of being naive and rustic. I feel it is plain and simple honesty. This sprit of truthfulness and honesty is what is so attractive in Meera.

'Meera's life begins at five a.m. when she crushes the grass for her buffaloes and lights the biogas *chula* for cooking the fodder. Despite the new money that has come their way with the sell of a plot of land, Meera continues to carry out her duties and has not become a lazy *memsahib*. She prepares thick *chapattis* in the earthen oven and milks the buffaloes. Breakfast is a simple wholesome meal of *chapattis* and milk.

'After the children are off to school, she bathes the buffaloes with the help of her elder son, Ajay, until their bodies are as clean as a brand new slate. Her husband uses a tractor to plough their fields. She cleans her home and prepares *chapattis* for their afternoon meal, which they generally take with curd and *saag* (greens). The children have started indulging in savouries available in the new stores within the colony. They have even started experimenting with pizzas from the pizza outlet just outside the colony gate.

'Meera observes her children tentatively prepare for a life so different from the one their parents have always known. She does not grudge the invasion of modernity, accepting that change is a constant process in the evolution of humankind.

'Often, during moments of quietude, she does savour the remains of a swiftly vanishing era as she lies down in her charpoy to watch the million stars twinkling in the darkness of a still clear night. How long will this peace and tranquillity last?'

Thus ends a chapter of Ruby's annotations on Gurgaon.

Pranjal experiences a minor tremor in his heart. An alien sense of shame snakes through his being and he is ashamed to recognize his newly cultivated arrogant deportment. He imagines his mother making a similar study. Ma, who had consciously laboured to bring him up to be a caring individual. How strange that he should fail to acknowledge the presence of the youth who delivered their milk every morning, let alone try to take an interest in his life.

Stranger still, that it is Ruby who makes an effort to understand them. Ruby, whose mother's life revolves around hosting the best party in the city. Pranjal feels almost as superficial as the haughty Mrs Gohain, his mother-in-law.

'You surely are the very breath I desire to breathe now and forever.' Pranjal declares embracing Ruby, drowning himself in her sweet heady scent, thanking all the powers above for bringing Ruby into his life.

Meanwhile, Ruby's apprehension of the petty nature of the wives of some of the so-called city dwellers inhabiting the complex proves right. A neighbour, who is the wife of an executive working in another organization, slyly conspires to create undue havoc in their lives by brainwashing the illiterate Dhani. She encourages her to cut down on the time she spent in the house. She lures Dhani with promises of much better prospects. She then pays Dhani a paltry sum of rupees fifty an hour for giving her a full-body massage, sealing her to a faith akin to slavery.

Ruby was big-heartedly paying Dhani five thousand rupees monthly, plus all meals and bountiful perks. However, the much academically qualified neighbour egged on the uneducated Dhani to lie. So, on the pretext of purchasing vegetables, Dhani would vanish for hours. She had a basket load of excuses handy.

When Ruby got a whiff of Dhani's misconduct, she initially simply cautioned her, 'Dhani, ask me for anything you need. I will try my level best to give it to you. Remember, never lie to me. Lying is the worst human failing. It destroys trust, the very foundation any relationship is based on. Also remember, I shall terminate your service if you ever betray my trust.'

'*Didi*, would I ever lie to you? You are my *annadatta*. I will never betray you. You are my God's messenger, who has come to save me from sadness and poverty. How can you even think that I will ever betray you?' Dhani had responded then.

Two weeks later, another neighbour rings and asks Ruby about Dhani's whereabouts.

'Why do you want to know whether Dhani has come or not?' Ruby enquires. 'She comes to your house for massaging you every alternate day? Really? She massages you for an hour and you pay her fifty rupees for every session?'

When Ruby questions Dhani the next time about the reason for her absence, Dhani persists on deceiving her.

'Dhani, I need you to work sincerely here. If you do not have time to manage all the work allotted to you, you should tell me so that I can employ an additional help. I am having difficulty coping with the extra housework due to your inconsistency. My work is suffering and I cannot afford it.' Ruby gave her many opportunities to come clean.

'*Didi*, how can you talk of employing another onc when I am already working for you? I will be regular from tomorrow,' Dhani promises.

'Will you Dhani? I am quite tired of your promises. Tell me honestly Dhani, are you working somewhere else? Is it that you need to earn more money than what I am paying you? You have to be honest with me. I need a full-time help. You know very well that your working hours are from nine to five. I require a help around those hours even if it is merely to answer the door. If you are not satisfied with what I pay, tell me now.'

'Promise *Didi. Ma kassam.* I am not working for anyone else. You are paying me full-time salary. What more can I ask for?' Dhani declares.

'No more *chhutties* (holidays), then. You learn to get all your personal work done on Sundays when you get your off day. Is that clear?'

'Of course *Didi.* None of the other house cleaners get a regular holiday every Sunday, as I do. I will never lie to you.'

Just then, the phone rings, 'Mrs Kumar? Dhani? She comes over to massage your body? Really? At twelve o'clock every alternate day, is it? You are aware that I have employed her as a full-time help? Pardon? You feel she is poor and that is why she needs to earn more money? I absolutely agree with you Ma'am. If you feel she can earn more you must employ her. Bye Ma'am.'

Ruby switches off the cordless phone before speaking to Dhani.

'Dhani you are working in three other houses during the time you are supposed to be working in my house. I have paid for your time for nine to five. If you feel what I am paying you is not enough then you should tell me instead of lying to me and sneaking out to work in another place without completing your duties here. It is unethical to cheat and tell lies, Dhani.'

'But *Didi,* I am poor. I need to earn,' Dhani says.

'Of course you need to earn, Dhani. Only, you must learn to earn honestly. There is no limit to our wants, and the more wants we can fulfil, the better for us. However, we must fulfil those wants through honest means. I am so sorry Dhani to lose you in this manner. After working for me for almost three years, I had thought that I could trust you. I had hoped I had satisfied your material wants and that you would never have to stoop down to telling lies.'

Dhani betrayed Ruby's precious trust to earn an extra fifty-rupee note. Even if she laboured in three houses and managed to earn six hundred rupees per month per house, it all added up to a grand total of rupees eighteen hundred only. No other benefits. She had connived to earn that additional money by skipping a major chunk of the work everyday for which she received an enviable amount. It is unlikely that this lesson will teach her to feel ashamed of being a cheater. After all, she genuinely believes it is smart business sense to hoodwink the employer for a few rupees more.

'Why? Why do women do it to themselves? Why is it so hard for one woman to accept another woman's conduct without wasting her energy scheming to pull the other down? You guys do not devote quite so much energy maligning one another,' Ruby despairs.

'Perhaps. But in this case even Dhani is equally to blame,' Pranjal points out.

'I guess it is the absence of a sense of permanency that makes them so susceptible to cheat and lie, secure in the knowledge that they are here for a limited time period. This sense of impermanency in the city unleashes their worst traits,' Ruby says.

Dhani lived to repent in leisure as she went back to her life of poverty and hardship. The money she earned was not enough to eat nutritious meals required for the strenuous task of a masseur. The three years she spent in Ruby's home were the golden period of her life. During this period, she had money to pay regular house rent, sufficient food to feed her family three square meals, sweetmeats and new dresses for everyone during festivals, a cooking gas for convenience and a brand new cooler to keep them cool during the long, hot, dusty summer months.

Ruby, on her part, learnt it the hard way that one needed to be street savvy rather than compassionate to get work done. She discovered that a generous person is often equated to being a pushover. The status of a respectable human being Ruby wished to elevate Dhani to lay shattered for it had no value for one who could not think beyond a few rupees more.

The day Ruby dismisses Dhani from service Pranjal goes out to the lounge bar he had frequented as a bachelor. He needs to get away from the house for a while: he cannot take the tension.

'I'll be back in an hour,' Pranjal calls out from the door.

'See you,' Ruby responds to the closing door. She redirects her concentration on scouring the yellow pages for an agency to find a new help.

'My. My. Look who is here… a saint in sin city!' Anita greets Pranjal. 'What's up? Trouble in paradise already?'

'I'm only here for a drink, Anita.' Pranjal, however, does not object to her joining him.

'So tell me, what are you doing here alone? I distinctly remember you proclaiming that you two did everything and went everywhere together. You two are not too well glued together now, are you?' Anita probes.

'It's nothing of the sort. I have just come here for a drink. I am leaving straight after I finish this,' Pranjal says. The last thing he needs is an inquisition by Anita. He is reluctant to seek answers even within himself for fear of facing his own faults and failings.

'OK. I am not one to accept responsibilities.' Pranjal grudgingly admits to himself. 'I'm not accustomed to looking after anyone 24 x 7.'

'Poor Pranjal!' Anita coos. 'It must be getting tough to keep pace with Miss Perfection, no? Waiter, get us another drink here.'

'I don't think...' Pranjal begins to decline Anita's offer.

'Just another one. Won't get you drunk.' Anita speaks persuasively. 'Stay Pranjal. We haven't talked for months. Remember how we used to drink the night away discussing your ambitions?' Anita smiles at the memory.

'Was a long time ago. I guess every youngster has dreams.' Pranjal returns her smile.

'Is it all that you imagined it would be, Pranjal? By opting to marry a girl from your own community, are you blissfully happy?' Anita asks.

Pranjal wonders. 'Am I happy? Right now, I want nothing more than to get away from all those responsibilities that come with being a husband. Duties of a householder can be a burden. I wish to remain carefree. But I am happy at home when domestic problems do not raise their ugly head.'

'One cannot be happy all the time. Happiness and grief criss-cross all the time in one's life,' he replies warily.

Nonetheless, he felt good having Anita fuss over him. At that moment, he felt Ruby was too wrapped up in managing their home in clockwork precision and was neglecting in taking care of him. He did not feel it was his responsibility to lend a helping hand to Ruby until they found a suitable replacement to Dhani. He was still petty-minded enough to consider only of his emotional well-being.

Chapter 9

After reading about Pavan, Pranjal makes an effort to answer the doorbell and take the milk in the morning. He seizes this opportunity to make small talk with Pavan. Pranjal is pleasantly surprised to discover that Pavan is a fine fellow—soft spoken, intelligent and hardworking. It is easy to see why Ruby is impressed by Meera's skills in bringing up her teenaged sons. Even Pranjal has seen boys going astray at this impressionable age. Besides, these are testing times for parents with teenaged children. Rajpal's nephew, Rakesh, is greying his mother's hair much before her time with his wild ways. Rajpal often voices his concerns about his nephew. Incidentally, it turns out that Rakesh is Pavan's classmate—same school, same class, same section.

Thereafter, Pranjal starts acknowledging Pavan's presence in the mornings. He is well informed on most happenings around the neighbourhood. Pranjal wishes to know more about Rakesh's problem. He assumes that Pavan, being Rakesh's classmate, is bound to be able to throw some light into the situation. He broaches the subject on a Sunday morning.

'Pavan, you're not in a hurry to get back home, are you?' Pranjal asks.

'No Sir,' Pavan replies. Pranjal observes that Pavan is not as comfortable with him as he is with Ruby. She can make anyone feel relaxed in her presence. Nevertheless, Pranjal is determined to win him over.

'Good. Come and sit down.' Pranjal invites Pavan to join him in their terrace garden where he had been reading the Sunday papers. Pavan walks in with uncertainty, hesitant on how to decline Pranjal's offer, unable to voice a refusal. He follows Pranjal like the proverbial sacrificial lamb.

'Would you like a cup of tea?' Pranjal enquires refilling his cup from the teapot.

'No Sir,' Pavan refuses, 'I don't drink tea.'

'Here, have a cookie. You'll like them. They are good.' Pranjal offers him the plate. Ruby makes the best chocolate chip cookies. Pavan takes one.

'Thank you Sir.' Pranjal observes that Pavan is impatient to know the reason why Pranjal has invited him in.

Pranjal decides not to needlessly prolong his agony and gets straight to the point. 'Tell me about your classmate, Rakesh. How is he performing in school? His Uncle is worried because he is always getting into some kind of trouble or the other.'

'He is the one who invites trouble, Sir,' Pavan stresses rather forcefully.

'How?' Pavan sounds like he had personally bore the burnt of Rakesh's wayward ways.

'He thinks he owns the school. He is extremely spoilt. He comes to school driving a fancy car, always trying to show off his expensive gadgets to the girls. Only last week he got an HTC Diamond to school. His parents give him everything. And because he gets everything at home, he feels he can have anything in the outside world as well.' Pavan says disparagingly.

'So what is it that he cannot have?' Pranjal asks shrewdly, 'Is it a girl?'

'Yes.' Pavan designs to reply in a monosyllable.

'And…?' Pranjal realizes that Pavan really is not being very forthcoming. Just then, Ruby arrives with a bowl of rich green French beans, plump mushrooms, snow-white shallots, sunset-red, sunshine-yellow bell peppers, and orange hill carrots.

'Hey. Do you guys mind if I come and join you? Chopping vegetables alone when there's interesting company is sacrilegious, don't you think?' Ruby smiles.

Ruby's smile does the trick. Pranjal can see Pavan's tension ebbing from him as his body language changes. He is visibly relaxed. His facial muscles ease into a smile from the uneasy look of apprehension he was wearing earlier in Pranjal's presence. He appears positively relieved to see Ruby. His expression completely shatters any illusion Pranjal might have had of being successful in putting the boy at ease despite his apparently intimidating persona.

Pranjal's mind flashes back to similar situations from the past, when he was a child, when his father was alive. Invariably, a person would feel more comfortable in the presence of his mother's charismatic bearing than his father's unapproachable stance. The person's reaction would irritate him. He would invariably say something nasty to Ma. Her body would quiver with the impact of the emotional blow. She would tearfully rush to the washroom or empty the flood of her grief over the kitchen sink.

'Yes, there is power of life and death in our tongue.' Pranjal reflects thoughtfully.

Pranjal often sneaked behind her without her ever finding out of his being there. She would rinse her face, fold her hands in a quick prayer and go back to carry on with the business of life.

His father never discerned her sadness. He never tried to understand the unhappiness she camouflaged with her silence. He never saw her delicate face stained with tears. He was not sensitive to situations that upset her. He could not understand her pain. Looking at her unguarded defeated expression, Pranjal had wanted to hug her and offer her some solace. But he knew she would hate to discover that he had witnessed her moments of weakness.

She educated Pranjal with a profound insight on the importance of maintaining a positive attitude the day he returned fuming from school as a ten year old after receiving a scolding from the language teacher for a silly little mistake he had committed. 'When you feel so bad you block away the abundance of happiness that is floating in your direction as a blessing from God. So run and clean your face with water, you will wash away the hurt. When you egg on yourself to smile, happiness simply returns.'

His father's words and actions did not embitter his Ma. Ma philosophized that even the *Mahabharata*, the great Indian epic, did not condemn envy of being a sin but considered it a 'poor mental hygiene.' As a little boy, Pranjal believed he could wash away all the sad and negative emotions simply by cleansing his face with soap and water.

'Come, my dear…' Pranjal now invites his wife, 'perhaps you can find out from Pavan what ails Rakesh.'

'Aha, Rakesh.' Ruby nods sagely as she starts slicing the colourful array of vegetables on the wooden chopping board. 'So, how is Rakesh doing? Is he still chasing Meenu?'

'More aggressively than ever. Yesterday he got a diamond pendent for her. When she refused to accept it, he threatened her. Really, the chap is a slur to his family. Some day, I am going to teach him a lesson.' Pavan speaks passionately. Pranjal observes that all his earlier self-consciousness has faded.

'No Pavan, you don't have to teach him a lesson. That is the responsibility of the school authorities,' Ruby says firmly.

'Hah, Ma'am, do you think our school authorities are adequately equipped to concern themselves with these things? As it is, the teachers are always complaining of overwork and underpay.' There is a note of fatalism in Pavan's dismissive tone.

'But they surely must be taking some action. What about the counsellor? Has she suggested any remedial measures to his parents?' Ruby asks.

'His parents were called the other day and they were strongly advised to control their son. But what can Uncle and Aunty do? Uncle was a farmer before he became a rich man from the money he gained by selling several plots of his farmland. Both Uncle and Aunty are illiterate. They have never ventured out of their village; they are clueless about the outside world. Rakesh refuses to listen to them. He is always hanging out at the lounge bars and clubs. He drinks everyday, and he drives his father's car to school.' Pavan shakes his head.

'Why don't you invite him over here some day? I may be able to drill some sense into him.' Ruby suggests. 'I can imagine how difficult it must be for him. He is at an awkward age; he has to try to fit into a society that is so unfamiliar to the one he has been brought up in.

'Suddenly, he has to content with cosmopolitan culture hitting him in the eye. Practically speaking, it takes a number of generations for the educated to arrive at a level of urbane sophistication. We are being horribly impatient in expecting the youth to make instant adjustment to slip into the fast-changing urban scenario merely by making modern consumer products available for sale in the posh malls. I'm sure Rakesh is a misguided youth trying to act out a role to impress an uptown girl.'

'Don't bother with him. He is a bad one. Has no respect for anyone. He is drowned in the *nasha*—power of his father's money,' Pavan declares.

'Yeah. Right. But that money will disappear one day if he does not utilize it judiciously. Then what will he do? After all, his father has sold off most of his land for this money. His father does not work. And Rakesh is their only son, isn't he?' Ruby enquires.

'That is the problem. He knows he can bully his parents into agreeing to his demands. And he is quite aware that he can lead a comfortable life without working because the property the family has will easily see him through very comfortably.' Pavan says. 'I am telling you Ma'am, something bad is bound to happen to this boy.'

'But I would still like to meet him once. Do try to bring him over someday.' Ruby urges. Pranjal observes that his mother and Ruby are incurably optimistic about being able to put the wrong to right. How many times has he seen Ma help an erring youth find his or her bearing?

'I'll try Ma'am, but I can't promise.' Pavan responds. 'I should be going now. I have cricket practice from nine o'clock.'

'Yeah, you shouldn't be late,' Ruby agrees. 'Bye Pavan.'

'Bye Pavan. Thank you,' Pranjal adds.

'My pleasure, Sir, Ma'am.' Pavan makes a swift exit with the enviable energy of an athletic youth.

'Perhaps you should accompany Rajpal to the school and have a word with the school authorities,' Ruby suggests. 'It worries me—young boys going astray due to mixed-up notions of being cool. My take on Rakesh is that he is a confused youth.'

'I'll discuss the matter with Rajpal Monday morning,' Pranjal promises Ruby.

Chapter 10

Unfortunately, tragedy struck on Monday morning, even before Pranjal reached office. Rakesh had taken Rajpal's pistol from his office chambers and shot at a classmate. Just like that.

Pranjal receives a call from Rajvir who says that he would pick Pranjal up from his home; he and Rajeev being already on their way. Pranjal tells Ruby what has happened and rushes down to wait for his friends to arrive.

Rajpal is in police custody by the time they reach the school. The school premises looks like a crazy circus with the media descending upon the area in its full force, with their high-tech gadgets and eager reporters—all out to deliver the scoop fresh and first to their audience. They zoom in their cameras for that special effect while showing the probable scene of the crime. It is, after all, about gluing the viewer to the television set and notching the highest television rating points.

The friends rush to the police station. Rajpal's entire village appears to be present there. They meet his uncle at the gate. His uncle is an even bigger man than Rajpal's six-feet muscular built. It pains Pranjal to see him weep. Without wasting time, they proceed to meet the officer-in-charge.

'Thank God for small mercies! The boy will survive. The wound is superficial. We have just received a message from the hospital,' Ram Singh, the officer in duty, says. Ram Sing happens to be a distant relative of Rajpal and a colleague.

'What happened?' Pranjal asks Rajpal, who looks devastated.

'Rakesh took my licensed revolver from my office. I had given him my car keys last night. He said that he would take my new car for a spin within the locality. My home office keys were in that same bunch. He opened the safe in my office and took the loaded revolver. Apparently, he wanted to teach some boy a lesson.' Rajpal shakes his head. 'I don't understand how he came to know where I kept my gun.'

Rakesh's parents look even more distressed. His mother, Nirmala Devi, wipes her eyes with her sea-green *chunni*—an expression of total misery and shame clouding her bewildered face. Her husband is in an animated conversation with several relations who rushed from their homes to the police station as soon as they heard the news. Several of them are still in the crumbled *kurta pyjamas* they had slept in.

This unfortunate incident is the beginning of a series of misfortunes that would strike Rajpal's life this ill-fated year.

The shootout incident turns out to be a murky issue, worsened by the extensive media coverage. Every aspect of Rakesh's life becomes topic of public discussion.

'True he had turned out wild, but he is still young enough to redeem his mistakes and start afresh,' Ruby says.

Ruby and Pranjal visit Rakesh at the juvenile home together. After several visits, Ruby starts to visit him alone. Initially, Pranjal is a little apprehensive of her venturing to meet him alone. He is frankly more than a little disturbed by the arrogantly appreciative way Rakesh earlier stared at her. The fact that he is a mere sixteen year old almost slipped Pranjal's mind for a moment. However, Ruby is firm in her resolve in instilling some sense into his young and irresponsible mind.

'Why are you so interested in my well-being, Ma'am? What am I to you?' Rakesh drawls.

'I could say you are like my younger brother but I really cannot, as I hardly know you. However, I wish to help you simply because you are a fellow human being,' Ruby replies.

'I don't need your help. I don't need anybody's help. I'm perfectly capable and grown enough to look after myself,' Rakesh smirks.

'It is an ever-changing world. And just when we are sure we have got it all worked out, we slip and fall. Then we realize we still need people to reach out to us. It has nothing to do with one's age or position in life. People need one another all the time, everywhere in the world. None of us is so omnipotent that we can pick up ourselves when we fall and not appreciate a helping hand that lifts us up to carry on with the business of life.' Ruby reasons.

'You think I need to change?' Rakesh speaks derisively.

'Even the best of us keep changing all the time; it's the process of evolution. I simply think you need someone to talk to, and I want you to know that I am here to listen to all your fears, uncertainties, ambitions and apprehensions. It does not matter what they are. I promise I will not judge you and dish out unwanted advice....' Ruby pauses and smiles, '...unless, of course, you want me to.'

It is a wonderfully rewarding feeling to see the transformation of a rebel into an almost well-behaved youth. Ruby has that power—to bring out the best in the people with whom she interacts.

Rakesh starts visiting them after serving his time in the juvenile home. He borrows books from Ruby and discusses the profound philosophies of Pluto and Socrates. And the wonderful reformation of a prodigal son takes place.

As time passes, Rakesh's rough mannerisms chisel into a polite behaviour. These days he respectfully stands up from his seat to greet Pranjal and addresses him in a courteous manner befitting an educated youth.

That blatantly sexual stare he had assessed Ruby with the very first time they had met has gone. Instead, he looks at her in awe and behaves in an almost deferential manner towards her. He chooses to listen to her. Rajpal thanks Pranjal profusely for thus transforming Rakesh. Apparently, Rakesh no more wishes to discontinue his studies; he now wants to go for further studies.

Ruby informs Pranjal that she has already helped him fill the admission forms for an engineering college in South India.

'The change will do him good.' Ruby states. 'He is an intelligent boy and just needs proper guidance. I am confident he will do well in life.'

'You've dealt with Rakesh like a professional,' Pranjal remarks.

'A few years ago, Shankar was suffering from a similar trauma and I failed to comprehend the depth of his despair and he is no more,' Ruby sighs.

'Shankar?' Pranjal asks.

'My second cousin. He lived in our ancestral village in upper Assam. His father, Pradeep *da*, remained in the farm and looked after the land. He was a simple man—not very educated, not at all ambitious, but a very likable person. When I visited them during my holidays, it always felt like a big adventure,' Ruby sighs. 'The property was lush green. An inner circle of *tamul* (areca nut) trees and an outer circle of fruit trees like *jamun*, olives, mango and palm surrounded their sprawling house. There were two pools—one was used as a water reservoir and the other served as a fishery.' Ruby pauses before continuing, as if gathering her thoughts.

'Surrounding this green paradise were the paddy fields where Shankar and I walked around after breakfast. Often, Shankar would pluck a blade of grass and slit the stem to make an instant flute and play a beautiful tune.'

'What happened to him?' Pranjal asks.

'He performed badly in his matriculation examination. Pradeep *da*, who had always nurtured ambitions for Shankar, was very angry and was rather harsh on him. He warned him to mend his ways or leave the house.'

'Shankar was headstrong enough to disappear into the night without a trace. The family searched for him for years but no one knew anything about him. It was as if his identity had been erased from the face of the earth.'

'He must be somewhere! How can someone simply vanish?' Pranjal asks.

'There were rumours of his leaving the country, of having fled to the jungles… but no one has heard from him or of him ever since,' Ruby sighs. 'I wish I were there the day his results were out. We were best friends. If he had called me up once or if only I had called him up that day, I am sure I could have talked sense into him.'

'I am sorry,' Pranjal says.

'Yeah, well.' Ruby tries to smile. 'That incident had taught me that these problems demand swift action. That is the reason I was so impatient to meet and talk to Rakesh,' Ruby says.

How simple she makes it all sound. Yet, the truth is usually gloriously simple. Perhaps all Rakesh ever needed was a nudge in the right direction from someone who understood his inner turmoil.

'Ma always maintained that it is the responsibility of the teacher to nurture students to develop their aptitude to the fullest potential. That the true success of a teacher lay not in his or her ability to promote the intelligent and the hard-working students to perform brilliantly but to encourage and instil confidence in the average students to achieve the best they were capable of,' Pranjal reflects.

No student in Ma's class enjoyed the elevated status of intellectual superiority. She firmly treated every student equally. This is perhaps the reason why every student performed so well in her class. Pranjal never heard her complain about the lack of intelligence of any of her students. Every time when a student needed help in a certain subject, she gave him or her extra guidance during her free time. She never accepted money for those extra classes, not even when she was going through dire straits financially.

After all, Pranjal's is the story of a 'below-average' student who made it to a premier institute of technology in the country when his professionally qualified teachers had given him up for a total failure. He won a place in the sun with a cushy job in India's shining upper strata—all due to Ma's unconditional love.

'Ma is a personality who brought me up with no pressure, no stress, no great expectations—by simply bestowing her unconditional love on me,' Pranjal says.

'There is no other way she could have instilled so much confidence in you,' Ruby agrees.

'The Admission Counsellor, the Buffalo (that was her nickname), had scorned at my aspiration. She was christened that name because of her obstinate and egocentric nature. According to her, my ambition bordered on audacity for I was not intelligent enough to apply for the PCM (Physics, Chemistry, Math) stream. Ma pointed out she was being biased in trying to prevent a student from pursuing the subjects of his choice,' Pranjal continues.

'Have you any idea how intelligent the students in my class are?' The Buffalo was their class teacher as well. 'Pranjal is a borderline student. How do you think he will ever be able to cope with the syllabus? Even intelligent students find it difficult to manage. I cannot risk the reputation of our school by allowing him to take up PCM. My suggestion is that if he is so interested in engineering, he can try to get into a vocational college after his boards. He can now opt for the commerce stream in the school and try his luck.'

'How can you speak so insensitively to a fifteen year old?' Ma asks. 'But I can promise you this on my son's behalf that my son will be the last person to sully the name of your school.'

Fortunately, for Pranjal, they had a gem of a principal who used her discretionary power to let him study PCM. Ma promised to transfer him from the school if he failed to get a decent percentage in the pre-boards.

'However,' Ma says, 'when one door closes another invariably opens. Our job is to walk right into that door with hundred percent commitment.'

Her confidence in Pranjal's ability nudged him to give the examinations his best shot and he passed the boards with an excellent percentage. He also became the only student in the class to secure a seat at a major institute by scoring twenty-fifth position in the All India Engineering Entrance Examination.

Thereby, Pranjal clearly demonstrated that ordinary hard work and determination could be worthier attributes than the prized gift of superior intelligence. He is now confident that it is possible to transform himself to the man he wanted to grow up into. Ma had guided him to discover the immense potential he had within him. No one can ever again make him feel small again, not even the Buffalo.

That was his first real taste of winning. It empowered him with confidence to embark on his journey into an adult from a young boy. Pranjal turned eighteen the year he joined the engineering college. Ma encouraged him to fly out of their cosy cottage into the wide world of independence, to soar as high as he wished.

Pranjal is conscious that Ma lugs a monumental baggage from having suffered discrimination during her school years. He knows that she missed studying in an excellent college in Delhi simply because a professor misinformed her about the cut off percentage for the hostel seat. Ma could not study in the capital without hostel accommodation. She had to abandon her aspiration to chase her dream of further studies for she was married off immediately after she returned home from Delhi.

She later learnt that the teacher waylaid her because she wanted to reserve the seat for one of her known candidates. Ma recounted this episode to Pranjal more than twice. She was, no doubt, trying to impress upon him the essence of intelligent trusting. Pranjal soon discovered that the average individual always has selfish interest to satisfy. He learnt to trust judiciously.

'Yeah, while it is true that a good teacher helps shape so many of his or her students' lives, even as individuals, we all have the ability to assist someone similarly simply by reaching out. A helping hand should not be bound within a structured framework. It should become so much a part of us as to become an involuntary action,' Ruby concludes.

Chapter 11

It is a cold, winter night, with dense fog menacingly looming, aggressively eating into their space, curtailing their vision of the world around them. On such a night, Ruby and Pranjal sit with steaming hot cups of chocolate in the garden. Ruby offers Pranjal her new short story to read while she sits down comfortably to write a travel piece on the Pushkar *mela* (fair).

The sanctified Pushkar Lake in the town of Pushkar is the site where Pushkar *mela*, the vibrant gala fete, is celebrated. Pushkar lies in the Ajmer district of Rajasthan state in western India. It is one of the most colourful festivals of India. Here men buy and sell their camels, cattle and sheep. The women purchase bracelets, cloths, textiles and fabrics. A camel race starts the festival. It is an exhilarating event for Ruby to pen down a dazzling travel feature.

They decipher the words by the light of kerosene lamps that Ruby had hung aesthetically to adequately illuminate the garden. An old-fashioned *chula* (clay oven) she had sourced from Shillong flames merrily to offer warmth. In Shillong, a hill station in the North East region of the country, *chulas* are used for boiling water and even cooking, apart, of course, from their fundamental purpose of offering warmth. As the fuel used here is coal, lighting up a *chula* within the closed confines of a room can prove lethal because of the high level of carbon monoxide emissions.

For Ruby, creating an appropriately conducive atmosphere is important in order to reap the optimum pleasure from reading a story. As the heavily moisture-laden air seals them within their cocoon, Pranjal begins to read the story *My mother and a Bowl of Rice*:

> My story is about my mother. She is the root of my existence, the rationale why I perceive the world the way I do.
>
> Yeah, I still think a lot about my mother's happiness. Ever since Dad's plane crashed when I was a ten year old, it has always been just Mama and me. She is a teacher at a Central School. I remember Dad's mom, my grandmother, whom I address as *Aita*, being awfully nasty to Mama whenever we visited *Aita*'s home. She said that Dad died because of Mama's bad luck.
>
> Even Mama's own family turned very formal overnight after Dad passed away.
>
> When Dad was alive, it was quite the done thing for Mama and me to occasionally go over and spend a few days in their house whenever Dad was out of station. They came to stay with us during my school vacations. Those were happy family days when I basked in the love of so many relations. Unfortunately, all of them faded away to the recess of my memory as the years rolled by after Dad's demise. Mama tried to maintain contact with both the families, but it was a difficult task. It was apparent to me even at that tender age.
>
> I sensed the difference. I remember visiting my mother's childhood home after Dad was no more. I had never

thought of her childhood home as being separate from her adult self. Since she was hurting and lonely she needed her family more than anything else. Yet, we were cordially received as guests that day and during our subsequent visits. We were steered and seated in Grandmother's massively spacious, ornately decorated drawing room and offered snacks and tea. I sat unnaturally, primly observing my beautiful mother discomfited by the turn of events. Ever polite and gracefully composed, she tried to hide from me that she was upset.

Later, she treated me to chocolate chip ice cream at our favourite ice cream parlour. We did not talk about how all our relations had changed in their conduct towards us. Mama did not want me to feel the change. She was extra cheerful at the ice cream parlour, cracking jokes and making me laugh until tears rolled down my cheeks.

I promptly forgot that it was my first visit to her childhood home, as far as I can remember, when Grandma did not indulge me with my favourite chocolate ice cream. During our rare subsequent visits, I never again enjoyed ice cream in their house.

I do not recall precisely when I started thinking of my Grandparents as different people—as not immediate family, or when I first started looking upon this world with its mind-boggling presence of people as housing only one close relation—my mother.

My eternally elegant, always understanding, forever caring, wonderful mother. I feel blessed that I have my mother always to fall back on. How did I know that she would never abandon me as her mother had so obviously let her down? I knew it not merely because we have only each other for support but mostly because we understand and believe in each other.

I learned early in my childhood that rock-hard trust and honest commitment is the ultimate foundation of any relationship.

I know my mother can never depend on Grandma to stand by her unconditionally, simply because Grandma does not care more about Mama than she does about her many societal values.

I have heard relations speak within my earshot how bothersome it is to have a widow and her son visiting their home. I have heard my mother's own father urge her to refrain from visiting their home too frequently. They were ashamed of us. They wished to maintain a distance from us so that they did not have to answer too many uncomfortable questions to other people.

Fortunately for me, my mother always has that ability to make me feel totally protected under her care. Even to this day, when I am a man, husband and would later become a father, I continue and shall always continue to cherish the feeling of fulfilment that my mother's presence has the power to invoke. At no time in my life, not even when I was a below-average, borderline student in school, did she make me feel unappreciated.

She loved me even when I performed badly, declaring rather dramatically in a grand tone that 'marks did not make a man'. In retrospect, it is this infallible confidence in me that she boasted of in her light-hearted banter that always made me strive for excellence. Her pure love in her action and practice has shaped me into a whole and happy individual.

There is definitely a vital distinction in the method in which Mama's mother, *Anna* has brought her up and Mama's style of bringing me up.

Anna continued to treat Mama perpetually like a child, in which she expected Mama to obey her every order without question. Yet when difficulties befell upon Mama, *Anna* was never around to help her. Conversely, Mama always encouraged me to voice my views. She listened to my opinions with utmost respect even when I was small. So even as a little boy I felt I had something important to say whenever I spoke.

Mama has not at all times agreed with my views, but she never belittled my opinion like the way *Anna* passed sarcastic comments on everything Mama said and did. Then again, Mama never imposed her opinion upon me. She merely tossed suggestions at me sometimes, but she persistently made it very clear that there was no obligation on my part to bow down to her wishes. Most importantly, she is always there for me as my mother whenever I need her whether I am thirteen or thirty.

The dissimilar upbringing of their children is more of a generational difference than a gender issue. I am confident Mama would have brought me up with as much love and care had I been her daughter.

Although I have moved to Gurgaon from Guwahati for better career prospects, I visit Mama every two months. Though she never once mentioned it, I know these visits are the highlights of her life.

She keeps herself busy with her schoolwork, giving tuitions to the weaker students and bringing out a bimonthly literary magazine.

She restricts her visits to the families, venturing to make the customary trips during festivals. She always keeps her visits short and formal. She has learned to distance herself from the familiar bonhomie she enjoyed with the families during the days before Daddy died.

Mostly, when my mother's memory washes over me like a soft cloak of comfort, what comes to my mind is a bowl of rice. I must have been all of two years old when the incident occurred. Yet, the vividness with which the incident has remained embedded in my mind is as clear as if it actually occurred today.

I was born under the caesarean section. After my birth, my mother had various health complications for which she was under medication for many years. Mama is a tall and well-structured woman. Therefore, she looks fit even when she is unwell.

I recall a beautiful summer day. Mama had completed the housework and prepared lunch, a simple fare of steamed rice, yellow *dal* (lentil) and a slice of fish. Mama fed me first. She fed me with her fingers, de-boning the fish and messing up the food to a soft pulp so that I could eat with my toothless gum. Just as she completed feeding me, Papa's Mama, my *Aita*, walked into the house.

Mama brought her a plateful of rice, a bowl of *dal* and a slice of fish. She quickly sliced a lemon and a cucumber, spooned some salt, washed some green chillies, and arranged them all in a plate for *Aita* to help herself. She rushed back to the kitchen to peel a potato and slice an eggplant into plump round slices and fried the vegetables rubbing them first with a little salt and turmeric powder. After *Aita* had eaten, Mama brought out a small bowl of rice with a little *dal*, announcing, 'I am so hungry. I hope you don't mind my eating now, in your presence.'

'You are bound to be hungry, of course. Look how fat you have made yourself stuffing yourself with my poor son's hard-earned money,' *Aita* said.

I do not think I will forget the look of pain in my mother's eyes as long as I live, even though I was then just a little boy. She looked so devastated. She did not reply. She quietly went and threw the bowlful of rice in the garbage bin.

That incident remained imprinted in my mind to haunt me throughout my adult life. If I had been a grown up, I would have objected to *Aita* for being so rude to Mama. All I did was cling to Mama. She lifted me on her lap and cooed me to sleep, singing my favourite nursery rhyme.

Every time I watched my mother chew her meagre meal with contemplation, I felt my heart constrict with an inexplicable pain. Every morsel she chewed appeared to stick to her throat as she swallowed determinedly. The bowl of rice that I had always associated with the sublime comfort of a mother's womb turned into a bowl full of wriggling worms in my mother's eyes.

When I grew up, I promised myself I would only marry the girl whom I would wish to cherish and treasure all my life. It is easy to fall for a pretty face. However, would I desire to fulfil her needs every day of our lives? Even when we were old and ill? So many women involuntarily serve and adjust in every situation, swallowing their pride, their self-respect, even their individuality—simply to maintain family harmony.

I promised myself I would never marry a woman until I was totally sure of my readiness to support her in every circumstance where she would need me. I do not think I ever forgave my father for not standing by Mama when she needed him to provide emotional, mental and physical strength. All he had to do was offer his support so that she did not have to face up to the family all by herself. However, he avoided confrontation with any of his family members and she became the punching bag for them all.

I know I shall not marry until I feel so close to my fiancée that I can experience her pain. It is easy to be in love in good times but to offer your wife your unshakable support when she requires it is what cements a relationship. Throughout her married life, I only saw Mama give and serve and slave to fulfil all her duties. I never once saw my father hold her in his arms and console her omit, let alone stand up to protect her. For him everyone else's feelings mattered except hers.

When I was nine, Mama became very ill. She had to undergo surgery. The following day after she returned home, both the families turned up for dinner and she cooked for them all. I helped her very little, but I was the only one who helped her. Perhaps she did not require their help but it would have been kind of them to stop maligning her at least for a day.

'It must be so hard on you, Dipankar… to put up with a sick woman. You poor darling. Come over to the club tomorrow, and join us for dinner. It will take your mind off all this depression,' Bani, Mama's portly cousin, said.

Mama was not a sick woman. She had just been ill and had had an operation. Where was the need for Dad to be depressed? As far as I observed, Mama had not inconvenienced anybody, even when she was ill.

'Thanks, Bani. That sounds wonderful. I must say, living with a sick person does make me most uncomfortable at times. I feel trapped in my life,' Dad said.

As a very young boy, I understood it required a man to be a mature, responsible and an honest individual to discharge the duties of a husband.

I love my father but I would have held him in great respect had his behaviour been different towards Mama. His memory sits heavy on my shoulders. His absolute loyalty to his family and never consulting Mama in any decisions left her vulnerably alienated.

Mama merely received instructions on how to carry out various tasks according to the wishes of his family. If she voiced the slightest doubt, she faced the threat of expulsion from the house the rented house, Dad, Mama and I lived in.

When I turned two and half, I was admitted to prep school. Mama joined the school as a nursery teacher and pursued her B.Ed. degree to equip herself with a teaching qualification. That way, she had her teacher's post in the Central School to fall back on. Becoming a teacher gave her an excuse to be out of the house. From seven a.m. to three p.m., the family could not interfere in her life. In the evenings, she taught me and helped other students as well. Thus, her life somehow shaped into a coherent whole.

In fact, it was with a loan, which she repaid from her salary, that she purchased the cottage, our home. She let *Aita* take all the official reimbursement due to her as my father's widow to avoid the spiralling torrent of *Aita*'s prejudiced allegations. However, *Aita* never ceased abusing Mama. My mother maintained her silence.

I am glad that the bowl of rice acted as a catalyst in motivating her to take a practical step towards reality. Even as a young child, my entire being rebelled against the manner in which Mama was mistreated. However, like so many women all around the world, she was hell bent on safeguarding a congenial atmosphere at home, refusing to take off those rose-tinted glasses with which she insisted upon envisaging the world. She loved Dad and no sacrifice was too great to remain with him.

Her occupation as a teacher enabled her to utilize her time and energy constructively. It was undoubtedly a blessed break to be able to steer young minds and show them the way towards a more meaningful life.

In return, Mama's job blessed us with the security of a home of our own. She was able to repay the loan from her own salary, without borrowing from any of the family members from either side. Her job provided her with a charming home, adequate food and the ability to support my education without requesting a relation for a loan. Most importantly, it changed the manner in which mother now chewed the bowl of rice.

Mama has always had a small appetite so instead of a plate she generally ate her midday food in a small bowl. Only when I turned ten and we started eating our meals together did she start serving her meals in a dish. She never again choked her food. It resumed its rightful position of being the sublime comfort that nourished our body and soul.

I figure that Dad's untimely demise and the inconsiderate humiliation Mama had to face due to our inferior social and financial status made me very aware of the importance of a solid financial standing in society. I was always very conscious that I needed to make a mighty tidy sum to help me maintain what I considered to be a standard lifestyle, throughout my life.

I have never lost focus on establishing an enviable status in the society. The years immediately after Daddy's expiry, Ma and I became invisible to the world around us. We rarely received an invitation to attend any function anymore.

Once I amassed wealth and property, became somewhat famous by winning a coveted national prize, we became visible to humanity as we know it today, again.

Everyday in every way I diligently ascertain that I am progressing in my life. Prosperity, fame and an enviable social network determine my definition of progress.

As for Mama, she happily accepts the small gifts I source for her from across the world as I quench my wanderlust. However, she refuses to accept anything expensive even from me. Initially, I resented her refusal to accept the things I had wished to give her all my life, at least as soon as I started to miss Dad's presence in indulging her as all the men in other families pampered their wives. Later, I learnt to respect her decision, her wish to clutch on to her sense of individuality.

Pranjal put down the printed file. He looked at Ruby concentrating on her work. She has this ability in totally losing herself on a task, living each moment as deeply and blissfully as a prayer. Pranjal thanks the Gods above for helping him discover such a wonderful individual to love.

Ruby glances at him and smiles. Closing her file, she asks, 'So, what do you think?'

'As always, I have to admit that you are an immensely perceptive writer. You have understood my predicament better than I have ever been able to decipher myself,' he says. 'The story reads like a humble offering to all the mothers across the world.'

'Thank you.'

However, there is an underlying uneasiness that Pranjal experiences after reading the story. Was Ruby in any way harbouring doubts about his reasons for marrying her? Did she suspect that he had married her to elevate his status in the society? After all, her family is one of the most well-known families in Assam.

'A writer's work is to look at a seed and observe it minutely from every angle. Then begins the creative process of imagining how it will grow when planted in a particular location, and how the tree will bloom, flourish, mature and finally take its last bow from the face of this earth. Surely, you have skilfully executed this creative process as a fine author. A creative individual needs to dip into his or her immense repertoire of insights within the self and create such characters that are realistic enough to convince the reader that they are more real than fictitious.' Pranjal, however, cannot restrain himself from praising her.

'I am so lucky to have you in my life. I just can't help wishing joy for the woman who created a perfect human being like you for me to love,' Ruby answers.

'I am not perfect, Ruby,' Pranjal replies very seriously. He does not want her to be shocked at any period of her life.

'For me you are what perfection is,' Ruby says simply.

'But it is dangerous to think of one's spouse as a perfect human being. I may not be able to live up to your high expectations.' Pranjal says, desperate to caution her.

'Who said anything about living up to my high expectations? My expectations are firmly based on my assessment of your character. I know the person you are. I love your intelligence and your good looks but I also love that balding patch on your thinning hair and your pathetic attempt at trying to be the life of a party,' Ruby says. 'Do you really think I am so immature that I would expect an unattainable icon of perfection for a husband? I am quite aware that I married a man, not a God.'

'Well, that's a relief to hear,' Pranjal smiles.

Will Ruby remember that he is only human when she discovers that he has married her as much for her lineage as for her charm? Pranjal wonders. 'She is so independent and individualistic. But how will I explain to her that the person I fell in love with comprises the total package of her individual characteristics as well as her family background?'

Chapter 12

Early next morning the incessant ringing of Pranjal's cell phone rudely awakens him. It is Rajeev. 'Rush to the Palm Springs Hospital. Room number 305. Rajpal has been shot,' he hangs up before Pranjal can articulate a response.

Pranjal looks at the number of missed calls. Seven. All from Rajeev, within the past two hours. Ruby and Pranjal had been dead to the world with exhaustion. Pranjal looks at Ruby sleeping peacefully like a little girl. It is five o'clock. He leaves without disturbing her.

At the hospital, it is a scene of total commotion. Rajpal's family has turned up by the truckload. All his relatives, in fact the entire village, appeared to be present. A group of women is consoling his mother. His wife appears relatively calm. Rajpal's father is in tears. Pranjal moves close to him, and he looks at Pranjal through the blur of tears and recognizes him. He grabs hold of Pranjal in an embrace, crying, 'Oh *beta*, look what they have done to our Rajpal!'

Rajeev appears within Pranjal's vision and he quickly erases the distance between them with his fast pace.

'Come with me,' Rajeev says.

Pranjal follows him into the room, his mind unable to take in the enormity of the situation. He has no idea as to what exactly he had been expecting even after having witnessed the mayhem outside. Rajpal recovering from a bullet wound, perhaps. Certainly not Rajpal breathing his last, wanting to have a word with him. Rajeev drags him by the arm beside Rajpal's bedside when his legs firmly root themselves to the spot he is standing. Rajeev pushes Pranjal's stubbornly stock-still head forward so that Rajpal can communicate the words he wishes to tell him.

'Thank you Pranjal, for being a good friend,' these are the faintest words Pranjal has ever heard uttered. Those were Rajpal's last words. Pranjal had always considered Rajpal's conduct melodramatic in life. It was astonishing that their friend left them just as dramatically.

It has been a long time since Pranjal had seen the life of a loved one end, not since they flew his Dad's body to their house when he was a ten year old. That was over twenty years ago. He was then too young to hurt too much for he failed to comprehend the finality of death.

As Pranjal watches Rajpal's life distance from him, with the Doctor beside him, the surrealistic truth of existence strikes him. The events that unfold appear hazy as he feels his soul momentarily leave his body to wander around aimlessly to try and decipher a reason of human existence. He watches people crying, mourning and grieving. He walks out of the hospital and sits in his car. Dazed.

The morning sun is bright in the sky. Too bright. The wailing—too loud. Life is a little too much at that moment to tolerate.

His cell phone rings. It is Ruby. 'Ruby,' he utters her name and cries.

'Where are you?' Ruby asks.

'The Palm Springs Hospital,' Pranjal replies.

'I'll be there in fifteen minutes,' she reaches him in fifteen minutes.

'It's Rajpal. He is no more,' Pranjal says.

Rajeev opens the back-seat door and lets himself in. He slumps on the seat and heaves a sigh.

'What happened?' Ruby asks him.

'Rajpal was shot by a terrorist last night. His colleagues brought him to the hospital critically injured. Everyone thought he would pull through. He was a tough guy and this wasn't the first time he had received a bullet wound. But this time fate had other plans for him.'

'Terrorist?' Ruby asks. 'Why would a terrorist want to kill a person like Rajpal?'

'Rajpal was an encounter specialist. Many of them were braying for his life. He led the anti-terror squad at the Delhi Mall last night,' Rajeev explains patiently. Pranjal had not mentioned the details of Rajpal's line of duty to Ruby because the occasion never arose but primarily because Pranjal wished to protect her from unnecessary apprehension.

'There was a terrorist attack last night?' Ruby enquires.

'For God's sake. What's with you guys? Don't you watch the news?' Rajeev asks impatiently. He does not know that last night they had been too busy with too many things to switch on the television.

'There was a terrorist attack at the Delhi Mall at around nine p.m. Rajpal had no information, just an uncanny calculated hunch he sometimes has, hence he and his men were also present there. Unfortunately, there were more terrorists than anticipated by the police. The scene last night was a bloodbath. Almost twenty people have died and over a hundred are injured.'

'How did he die?' Ruby breathes the words almost in a whisper.

'He was in a hurry. Anand, his son, is not well. Sushma *bhabi*, his wife, informed me Rajpal was planning to return early and take Anand to the hospital. Most likely, due to this preoccupation in his mind, he carelessly skipped wearing his bulletproof jacket. They hit him thrice during the encounter. But he managed to kill two terrorists and injure another,' Rajeev says.

Rajvir joins them and slouches down on the back seat beside Rajeev. Rajvir looks dishevelled. He had been with Rajpal all night. Rajvir's loss was even greater for the two had grown up together: they were from the same village and had studied at the same school.

The entire men folk of Rajpal's village and those belonging to his wife's village turn up to the cremation grounds. Ruby stays back with the women at Rajpal's home. On their return, Pranjal finds Ruby sitting alongside Sushma on a bed, sitting with her legs crossed in a meditative posture and in earnest conversation with Sushma. The friends return home after completing the last rites of Rajpal.

Ruby and Pranjal return home almost in silence. They had both faced bereavement up close. But this is the first time they grieved together in losing a friend.

As is customary in their part of the world, Ruby lights a little lamp and offers a small prayer for Rajpal's soul before letting Pranjal into the house. Pranjal is a little taken aback when she tells him to remain outside until she brings the glowing *diya*.

'After our endless discussions on religion and your views on faith being beyond religion, I am surprised by your ritualistic act. But, then, you never cease to surprise me,' Pranjal says.

'This is a simple act of homage for the departed soul,' Ruby says. 'One does not need to be practising a particular faith merely to balance energies.'

'Will it balance the energy in Rajpal's household?' Pranjal asks.

'Of course it will balance the energies. You are there. How can anything wrong ever happen to his family when he has friends like you, Rajvir and Rajeev?' Ruby says.

'Tell me, would it have helped if Dad had a good friend to come to Ma's aid?' Pranjal asks.

'That is a hypothetical question. Ma managed to reverse her fortunes and you multiplied them,' Ruby says. 'But definitely, a reliable friend is bound to have made her struggle a little easier. At least I think so.'

'A reliable friend,' Pranjal says.

'I know it appears a redundant use of a trait with a term that essentially conveys that meaning. But nowadays, we tend to use the word *friend* so loosely that it is necessary to deliberate upon its meaning,' Ruby says.

'I'll always remain a friend Rajpal can rely on even beyond his death,' Pranjal speaks passionately. He had experienced what it felt like to live without a good friend after his father left them.

'I know,' Ruby smiles understandingly.

They take a bath and then sit out in the garden. When Drishti, the new help, arrives, she brings them tea and biscuits. She senses a gloom pervading the atmosphere.

'*Didi*, has something terrible happened?' Drishti asks, placing the tray on the table. She stands with her hands folded in front of her.

'Something terrible has taken place, Drishti. A friend of ours was shot at last night along with many people by a terrorist in Delhi. He expired this morning,' Ruby responds.

'Oaf, these terrorists. All the time killing, killing. Why can't they just work hard just like the rest of us?' Drishti says.

'I don't think it is merely a matter of money. Not all terrorist are poor, Drishti,' Ruby says.

'If they have enough to eat then what is their problem? Why do they need to kill?' Drishti asks agitatedly.

'I don't know Drishti. Perhaps they are anguished misguided souls who have lost their basic human ability to decipher between the right and the wrong, perhaps they are so immersed in resentment and hate that they are unable to hear their voice of conscience, perhaps they have been so horribly brainwashed that they can actually qualify a reason for their heinous acts,' Ruby murmurs almost to herself.

'There is no excuse for killing,' Drishti states vehemently.

'No Drishti, there is no excuse for killing,' Ruby agrees.

'Should I cook lunch?' Drishti asks. 'I have to reach home early. I came here once in the morning but the door was locked.'

'It's almost evening. This tea is enough. You can prepare something simple for dinner if you have the time.'

'Okay, *Didi*. I'll see what I can manage,' Drishti says. 'There's the doorbell ringing. I'll check who is at the door.'

'Thank you, Drishti,' Ruby says.

'Rajeev*ji* has come. I asked him to come up to the garden,' Drishti announces within moments.

'Hey, Rajeev. Come and have a cup of tea. Drishti, please get another cup and saucer and the cake tin from the kitchen,' Ruby says.

'Okay, *Didi*,' Drishti says and reappears in a moment. The woman worked in the speed of lightning.

They drink their tea in silence. They even have a slice each of homemade chocolate cake. They had been too preoccupied to realize that they were hungry. They resume their conversation only after drinking their tea. It strikes Pranjal that they had been too exhausted emotionally and physically to even speak.

'Rajvir is taking this very badly. He has been drinking ever since we returned from the cremation ground. *Bhabi* is worried sick. He refuses to listen to anyone. I've just come from his place. That man refuses to get a hold on himself. We are all shattered at having lost Rajpal, but Rajvir appears hell bent on drinking himself to an early grave. He's unnecessarily exposing his weakness before his children,' Rajeev observes.

'I thought Rajpal and Rajvir did not consume alcohol in their homes,' Ruby says.

'Normally, no. However, at the moment Rajvir is anything but normal,' Rajeev says.

Pranjal calls Rajvir up from his cell phone. He takes his time to answer. When he finally does respond, his voice is slurred.

'Pranjal, tell me how can I carry on living without Rajpal?' Rajvir garbles. 'How can I continue living without my *yaar*, my *dost*, my friend? You understand?'

'Try to get a grip on yourself Rajvir. Life has to go on....' Pranjal starts speaking lamely.

Rajvir does not let him complete his sentence.

'Go on, go on. Hah, Pranjal where do I go on from here? Everywhere, everyday of our lives we have been together. Now where is there to go?' Rajvir demands.

'Rajvir, should I come over?' Pranjal asks.

'And do what? Watch me wallow in the depths of despair like a weakling?' Rajvir's voice is barely audible.

'I'm coming over.' Pranjal says before disconnecting the phone. 'Come on Rajeev, let's go. We'll be back soon, don't worry,' he assures Ruby.

Rajvir had taken the trouble to hide the bottles before their arrival. However, his mouth needed to be fumigated to sanitize it of the stench of the drinks he had been consuming. He is still wearing the white kurta pyjama he had worn to the cremation ground. He is alone in a room, yet the house is teeming with relatives and friends.

The room is probably a private sitting room. Pranjal had been to Rajvir's home only once before. During that visit, he had sat at the family drawing room, which was much more spacious and opulently decorated. This room is relatively smaller and the interior subtly elegant—a very different decor from what he would have expected Rajvir to be comfortable in. There is even a bookshelf with Hindi detective books arranged in neat rows. Teakwood chairs, tables and bookshelves are stylishly arranged in the room. On a wall is framed an aesthetically appealing shelf that displayed an array of remarkable showpieces from different parts of the country.

Pranjal and Rajvir have known each other over seven years. Yet, here appears to be much of Rajvir that he does not know. Entering this room, obviously Rajvir's personal domain, gives Pranjal an invaluable insight of Rajvir as an individual. On seeing him seating so forlorn in his room, Pranjal's earlier sentiment of slight annoyance at his total lack of control over his emotions entirely evaporates.

Then the stunning truth strikes Pranjal, overwhelming him with an urge to shield Rajvir from the monumental hurt he is experiencing. Rajpal had not been a mere friend of Rajvir. Rajpal epitomized everything Rajvir ever wanted to be in life but did not have the ability to become: Rajpal's strength, his daredevil attitude in confronting a dangerous situation, his total devotion to whatever he believed in and his unwavering loyalty to every cause he supported. Standing six feet three inches tall with an athletic built and the mental strength of a saint, he was the man Rajvir could never be. As in life, so in death, Rajpal would always remain his hero.

Simultaneously, another realization hits Pranjal. He realizes that it was not just Rajvir who hero-worshipped Rajpal, but that even he had trustingly looked up to Rajpal as an elder brother and unconsciously sought to emulate his enviable traits.

Rajeev and Pranjal sit down. Rajvir looks at them with bloodshot eyes. He rubs them with the back of his hand and says, 'Pranjal, you had to come and see me broken, eh?' his pathetic attempt to smile makes Pranjal wish he knew how to comfort him.

'You're too strong to let life break you,' Pranjal murmurs.

'Do you know Rajpal and I grew up together? He was born only a few months before me. We were neighbours. We went to school together. We went to college together. Then he joined Law College and I went to pursue my MBA degree. Yet there never went a day when we did not meet. Even when he joined the police service, no matter how late he returned from duty, we met regularly. There is not a single day in my life I can recall that I have not shared with Rajpal. My life has been broken Pranjal,' Rajvir sobs.

'Out of the four of us, Rajpal was the one always full of life. He was never an inactive spectator in any situation. He was always ready with a course of action to solve every problem, he was eager to get that extra bit more out of life; he wanted to experience existence to the core. I think despite his painfully early demise, his soul is content with having saved so many men by shielding them with his body. A brave person like him would not wish to go any other way,' Rajeev says.

'We should erect a memorial in Rajpal's name,' Pranjal suggests. 'I think that will help you heal your hurt. Why don't you start a professional college in his memory? Rajpal was a hero. I am sure the people in the village will be more than willing to help you in your endeavour. You're suitably educated. Establish an institute in his name and you run it. That way you will keep his memory alive. It will be an appropriate contribution of a true friend. And we are always there to help.'

'True. Very true. It will be an ideal gift for all that he was to me, for all that he has done for me,' Rajvir acknowledges. 'Thanks Pranjal for turning my train of thoughts from wallowing in self-pity at losing such a good friend to think constructively on establishing a centre of learning in the glory of his memory—a concrete tribute to our friendship. What a great thought.' Rajvir makes a valiant effort to smile. 'We are together in this, right Pranjal, Rajeev?'

'All the way,' Pranjal and Rajeev respond.

'Now I suggest you join your wife and children for dinner. Rajeev and I will come over tomorrow morning and together we will go to Rajpal's house. We can discuss the matter with his family. Will seven o'clock be alright with you guys?' Pranjal says.

'Seven. Fine,' Rajeev agrees.

Rajvir nods.

Rajeev and Pranjal depart.

The three friends find solace in their plan of keeping Rajpal's memory alive.

Chapter 13

Marriage and its accompanying sense of timelessness have made Pranjal a little careless in his duties at the office. Not that he has been shirking work—such laxity would spell doomsday notification for his career in their competitive setup, where someone is ever ready to malign one's reputation. There is always a fierce struggle for over half a dozen of them scrambling to ruthlessly grab a higher rank during promotions.

Promotions in the office can often be a mess. Recommendations arrive from all the concerned politicians. These references may be on caste basis, family relations and other equations that have absolutely no relevance to a candidate's professional performance. The bottom line is to keep the bosses happy or stay armed with adequate political or bureaucratic clout to counter the boss's decision.

Now, different bosses have different requirements. A particular boss may be satisfied with an executive being at his constant disposal; another one may expect officers to perform personal work, while a still different one may be on a one-man mission to promote personnel solely on regional, communal or caste prejudices.

One would presume that output goes for a toss when a company is so busy with politics. This is where people like Pranjal manage to squeeze in a foothold—by curving a niche that another executive cannot fill in, by making sure that he is completely indispensable when specific problems arise in the company. After completing his engineering, he did his MBA with specialization in personnel management. For that reason, he works in the human resource department, which suits him well. Being a predominately engineering company, the competition is relatively less in the HR department when it comes to promotions.

Pranjal's previous omnipresent boss would have given him a piece of his biased mind had he been around to notice his recent lackadaisical attitude towards his work. The only way Pranjal had managed to keep him from banishing him into a corner without work, thus rendering him useless for promotion, was by being the only person performing like a true pro in a department where everyone else was busy playing dirty politics.

That bugger belonged to an old school who believed that every individual from the North Eastern region was a terrorist come to slaughter the daylights out of him. The poor man initially made sure he was never alone with Pranjal, whose six feet muscular built and Mongolian eyes did little to reassure his uneasiness.

He hated Pranjal's guts. He failed to confront Pranjal when Pranjal refused to run personal errands for him and pander to his personal gratification. There were officers who went to the extent of shopping for groceries in order to remain in his good books.

'Who does he think he is?' Boss Intolerable cursed in frustration. 'If I could, I would transfer him this very moment.'

'Sir, best avoid him.' Mr Kumar advises with the wisdom of experience. 'He can create unnecessary ruckus for us. We will work out a plan to displace him. Only, it has to be done smoothly without raising his suspicion.'

'Well, think of a way to get rid of him Kumar—and fast.'

'Yes. Sir.'

The state of affairs in the office deteriorated to such an extent that Pranjal started sending his resume to a select few private organizations. He was seriously contemplating accepting a lucrative offer when the situation in the office took an unexpected positive turn for him.

Boss Intolerable failed to get the extension he was so confidently expecting. He left the organization one fine day just like another retired employee, with a strictly official farewell. Before he got his marching orders, he had behaved as if the organization belonged to him.

From being the Man of the organization where not a decision was taken without his sanction and not a leaf in the official gardens soiled in dust without raising his wrath, even his name is obliterated from the memory of all those who had worked and grovelled under him. Even his coterie abandons him as he steps down his elevated position.

How the mighty Man fell. Although Pranjal is the person he had detested the most, Pranjal is pained to see him fall. And so, Pranjal ventures with a bouquet of flowers to bid a personal farewell to the retired couple the morning they vacate their official residence. Blame it on an ethical upbringing by a perpetually socially conscientious parent. But he could not have lived in peace with himself by being discourteous to a senior when he was down and out. Pranjal finds he is not capable of such blatant misbehaviour.

There is no one else to bid the Big Man farewell, not even one of the many junior officers from his home state he had helped get into the company.

'I wonder where they bury their guilt. Perhaps the voice of their conscience is as incomprehensible to them as is the existence of their soul.' Pranjal contemplates, little realizing that he too would behave in a similar manner when the time came for him to choose between the truth and the probable truth.

Needless to add, every employee in their company is acquainted with the Krishna philosophy, of the individual soul being without a beginning or an end... and that 'no knife can cut it, no fire can burn it and no wind can blow it away.' After all, all employees and their families dutifully attend the religious rituals performed in the places of worship within the campus.

Yet no one fears the consequences of offending or shredding another's reputation, for that appears to be the current value system. The prevalent mindset dictates that only a loser would be foolish enough to go out of his or her way to be cordial to another without an ulterior motive.

Surprisingly, Boss Intolerable greatly appreciates Pranjal's humane gesture, particularly as it somehow salvages his battered pride in front of his wife.

His wife comments, 'What a perfectly nice gentleman Pranjal is!'

Pranjal's gesture is tantamount to committing professional hara-kiri. When word gets around, he is likely to be nicked off from the good books of the new boss when the prying eyes of one of his colleagues report of his calling on Boss Intolerable to bid him goodbye. There is nothing more dangerous for an executive than to be branded as one of the previous Boss's key men, particularly when the outgoing and incoming Bosses happen to be sworn enemies. Pranjal's action can spell a damaging debacle for him with his new boss.

He looks at Pranjal. 'What is he thinking in this particular moment?' Pranjal wonders. 'Perhaps that he had been too hard on me. Perhaps he thinks nothing at all. Who knows? Who cares? He is merely my ex boss now. Frankly, I do not wish to contemplate any longer on what went on inside that devious mind of his. What matters to me is that Ma will be proud of her son's act of bravery in such a sensitively volatile situation.'

Boss Intolerable was insufferable enough to scorn a suggestion Pranjal had volunteered as an unsophisticated executive. In his enthusiasm, he had put forward a proposal that could save the company crores of rupees. Pranjal was then too new to realize that a junior should not offer a suggestion unless specifically asked to voice his ideas.

Ever since that embarrassing episode, when Boss Intolerable sniggered at his naivety, Pranjal has kept the finest ideas to himself. He has discovered it is best to let the boss believe he is truly the Lord of all that he surveys. Only a fool who wants to be divorced from his post ever presents himself to be brighter than his boss. Pranjal convinces himself that he is but an insubstantial, formless, unimportant junior who even when present in the august presence of his boss, remain unseen. If he wished to regain his respect, Pranjal knew that he needed to be patient.

Once Mr Perfect Boss joined, Pranjal has had many opportunities to disgrace Mr Intolerable. He could delay his pension, his provident fund, he has the power to make him run an umpteen number of times for his medical bills… the list is endless. However, when the opportunity arose to take revenge, Pranjal found that he could not be bothered. From being a malignant growth, threatening to develop into a full-fledged cancer that could definitely be fatal, he became merely a cyst, which ceased to harm Pranjal after being removed by a simple surgery of forgiveness.

Pranjal's new boss is the Perfect Boss. He is easily the most intelligent amongst the lot. He is sophisticated and shrewd. Not even a thought can cross his junior's mind without him being perfectly capable of peering into it.

As if all his practical managerial qualities are insufficient to aid him in maintaining his position, he consolidates his stature by appealing to the Gods. He prays as awesomely as he works. His incessant fervent prayers leave the Gods no respite but to grant him his wishes. After invoking the Gods, he knocks at all the powerful earthly doors of relevant bureaucrats and politicians until they too, poor mortals, succumb under the might of his clever manoeuvring tactics.

He is the worst kind of enemy one could have the misfortune to make. Fortunately, for Pranjal, they meet on a common ideological platform. He is a thorough professional. As long as Pranjal is performing perfectly in his work, he knows that his Boss is satisfied. He does not expect Pranjal to run his household errands nor does he expect him to stroke his ego.

Pranjal could not have asked for a better boss to satisfy his self-esteem, which refuses to bow down to any mortal in submissive servitude. He is a smooth operator; he often consults Pranjal before he takes a decision. Not that he always acts upon his advice, but it elevates Pranjal's self-worth to know that the Boss values his opinion enough to seek his viewpoint before taking a decision.

Chapter 14

Anita's obsession with Pranjal ignites to an inferno by his lack of interest. It leads her to live under the delusion that Pranjal is actually camouflaging his love for her, that Ruby is just a passing fancy. Anita even manages to sway a few of their colleagues to her point of view. So, without even having met Ruby, many form the opinion that Ruby and Pranjal are not a happy and compatible couple. Pranjal is quite aware of the fact that given a chance they will pounce upon Ruby and present her with what they believe to be the true picture between Anita and him.

Despite Boss Intolerable's many faults, he was completely devoted to his beautiful wife. There was no scope of a female executive trying to get ahead in her career by fluttering her lashes at him. He was immune to the charms of all other women save those of his gorgeous Mrs.

Unfortunately, despite all the admirable characteristics Boss Perfect possessed, he did eye up the ladies. While Anita had maintained a safe distance from Boss Intolerable for fear of raising the wrath of Madam Intolerable, she lost no time in worming her way into the office of Boss Perfect. Anita quickly made herself indispensable by clocking in extra hours of work.

Pranjal's professional capacities paled in comparison against the might of Anita's undeniable charms.

However, Anita is not one to be satisfied with pocketing the most important departments and convincing Boss Perfect to prepone the date of promotions so that she can bag a higher rank early.

Pranjal maintains an unaffected facade to these minor developments. Matters come to a head when Anita manages to get the two of them nominated for a weeklong training together. Pranjal tries his best to convince Boss Perfect that it is unnecessary to send two executives for the training. However, Boss Perfect firmly instructs that he accompany Anita.

'Ruby, the training is in a Management Institute in Lucknow. Why can't you come with me? You'll enjoy visiting Lucknow. Lucknow has everything you enjoy—ruins, culture and a great cuisine.' Pranjal is aware he sounds desperate. What will conspire in Lucknow with Anita present? With Ruby by his side, it will definitely prove easier to maintain his self-control.

'And I would have loved to accompany you, Pranjal. But I can't. I've promised Mr Reddy that I shall submit the story by the weekend and I haven't even started research on it. Next time, Pranjal,' Ruby promises.

'But I want you to come this time. I *need* you.' Pranjal begs.

'Pranjal, be reasonable. I've already given my word. Won't you feel bad knowing I have not kept my word?' Ruby says.

'I won't feel bad at all.' Pranjal thinks. 'Of course, you must keep your word,' he mumbles.

'We'll visit Lucknow together another time. Promise.' Ruby smiles.

'Yeah. Sure,' Pranjal says shortly.

Anita cunningly arranges and occupies the seat beside him on the flight to Lucknow. Pranjal activates his laptop making it abundantly clear to her that he intends to work. She merely smirks and promptly falls asleep with her head on his shoulder.

'The campus is vast, green and isolated from the city. Ruby would have loved it here.' Pranjal cannot help thinking.

'Pran. This is wild. We are entirely alone here, away from all our friends and acquaintances. Isn't it exciting? We can do anything and no one would be any wiser. We can behave like a couple and no one would raise an eyebrow. We can pretend to be engaged or…' Anita rattles.

'Stop. Anita, stop fantasizing. I do not intend to let Ruby down, ever. The sooner you get that, the better it will be for you.' He takes a deep breath and modulates his voice to sound calm and unruffled. He does not intend to let her see how infuriated he is with her clinging presence. 'And stop calling me Pran. I don't like my name shortened.'

'Okay Pranjal, you be a good boy,' Anita smirks. 'Driver, get this five hundred rupee note changed from that store near the gate. Buy a packet of chocolates if they refuse to give change. Go.'

'How had I tolerated this pompous woman who treats everyone around her so superciliously?' Pranjal wonders morosely.

'His name is Gaurav,' Pranjal says, annoyed by her rudeness towards the earnest young man.

She turns towards Pranjal as soon as Gaurav leaves and kisses him hard on his mouth. He pushes her and walks out of the car without waiting for her, dreading the week ahead.

Anita has come well prepared. She wastes no opportunity to be close to Pranjal. No matter whom he is conversing with, she comes and joins them. She hangs on to Pranjal's every word, stands as close to him as possible and makes it embarrassingly clear to whosoever he is conversing with that that person's presence is unwanted at the moment.

'What do you want?' Pranjal asks exasperatedly, tired of constantly trying to fence himself away from her.

'You. Only you,' Anita declares looking at him with her amazingly big eyes.

All Pranjal needs to do is let himself go with the flow. He could excuse his reaction as involuntary and totally beyond his control. He had sought refuge on such white lies innumerable times before marriage.

Instead, his response to Anita's passionate entreaty is cool. It is as if his mind is embalmed with a calmness that has given him total control over his senses.

'Anita, come, let us sit down.' He gently invites her to sit down on a bench with him.

'Whatever you say, Pran,' Anita purrs.

'I hate cats,' Pranjal mutters beneath his breath.

'We need to talk.' Pranjal speaks firmly. 'Anita, you are bent on viewing me as a trophy to be won. If you were honest with yourself, you would admit that it is the sole reason you wish to be with me. You've convinced yourself that you need to conquer me because you feel Ruby has won me. It's just another assignment you need to pocket.'

'I was a part of your life before Ruby came waltzing in with her promise of a life you had always dreamt of. If she hadn't come, you and I would have been together,' Anita claims.

'No, Anita, we would not have been together. We have known one another for years, yet I never proposed marriage to you even once, doesn't that say something about my feelings for you?'

'You have always been ashamed to admit you loved me. Give my intelligence some credit. You won't have spent those endless hours in my company if you didn't care,' Anita remarks.

'The fact is we were good friends. I still value our friendship, but being in love is something totally different. It's much, much more than friendship. Anita, I'm sorry if at any point in our association I led you to believe that I was in love with you with any word or deed. I would never wish to hurt you.' Pranjal says.

'How do you know we can't be more than friends? We've never slept together, never made love. Maybe…' Anita whispers.

'No! Damn it,' he almost shouts. It was not his intention to insult her. However, her train of thoughts revolts him. Particularly, since he does not even have to close his eyes to see Ruby's alluring visage in his mind's eye. All his senses are fixated on Ruby and her radiance—her magical touch, her smell—not a mild floral fragrance, but the precious perfume of a garden abloom with scarlet roses—fresh with dew drops on a winter morning, her incredible body…. Her very presence arouses him into a trembling awareness of his insatiable hunger.

'Look Anita, love happens when you want to share all the joy life has to offer with that person. When you want to protect your loved one from all the sorrow life is bound to heap upon each and every one of us. When you want to spend every moment with that person and you feel incomplete when you are apart. I could never feel that way about anyone else but Ruby.'

'What has Ruby got that I haven't?' Anita challenges.

'I didn't consciously plan to fall in love with Ruby. Perhaps, when I learnt of her lineage I was overawed and set out to win her. But I cannot tell you when or how I fell in love with her. I guess we are born to love the ones we fall in love with,' Pranjal attempts to philosophize the situation.

Anita stares at him. 'Would you still love her if you lost your job?'

'Are you threatening me, Anita?' At that moment, Pranjal stops feeling sad for her. 'So far, I empathized with you. Unrequited love can be hell. However, planning vengeance on someone merely because the poor guy doesn't love you is gross. All I want is to distance myself as far away from you as possible.' Pranjal leaves her sitting on the bench.

Even as he walks away from her, Anita calls out. 'You are not so different from me, Pran. We have both used underhand methods to crawl our way up the ladder. The only difference is I am not afraid to admit my dishonesty while you are hiding behind a facade of honesty. You cannot erase your past, Pran. It is a part of you.'

Pranjal quickens his pace, desperately trying to escape from a past, of which he is speedily becoming ashamed.

How is he to find peace and happiness with Ruby if his inner turmoil threatens to destroy his peace of mind? He needs to come clean with Ruby. Unfortunately, the time never seems right for a confession.

Chapter 15

By his third day in Lucknow, Pranjal wants nothing more than the trip to end and return home to meet Ruby. He is tired of trying to avoid Anita.

It is almost dinner time. After that exchange with Anita during tea, Pranjal has locked himself in his room. He covers his face with his hands almost crying in frustration. He is aware of feeling and behaving more like a three-year-old little girl rather than a thirty-two-year-old man. He has never felt so helpless in dealing with any situation.

Someone is knocking at his door. He walks up to answer it and all his unhappiness, anger and frustration fly out into unknown space at the sight of the most wonderful woman on the earth waiting outside.

'Ruby!' He pulls her inside the room and embraces her with the urgency of someone trying to escape a furious forest fire eating its way hungrily towards him.

'You came!' He says much later when he can bring himself to let her breath again.

'I managed to complete my work before time. So I decided to surprise you.' Ruby's serene smile calms him magically.

'I'm gratified.' He says, knowing that she must have burnt the proverbial midnight lamp to be with him.

All at once, Lucknow emerged from its hazy background of neglected mausoleums of a bygone era to a dazzlingly romantic place on earth. At that moment Pranjal realises that no matter in which part of the world he lives his life, he wants Ruby always there beside him, sharing every moment, every experience and every dream.

They move to a hotel located close to the Institute. In the chilly evenings, after Pranjal returns from his training, they explore the city of the nawabs.

With the setting sun, the temperature drops drastically. As the evening progresses, the fog descends and encases the world around them enveloping them in a globe of their own. During the period of his training, they manage to go out for dinners only.

Therefore, they stay back another day in Lucknow after the training. In fact, they had planned to spend a couple of days exploring the area, but Anita on joining office manages to influence Boss Perfect that Pranjal is needed to attend a meeting within two days. Boss Perfect rings up Pranjal personally and orders him to return immediately to Gurgaon. Still, Pranjal and Ruby manage to make their last day in Lucknow a red-letter day.

They set off early to see the city. With Ruby thrilled as a little girl out to explore Disneyland, Pranjal finds some of her excitement rubbing off on him. The hazy sketch of ruins of minarets and domes of Islamic mosques, tomes and mansions stand testimony of an era of grandeur and the ruins of the Residency appear a portrait of the miasma of death. However, as the smog fades with the sunlight forcefully making its way upon the old city, the faded remnants of another period speak of a magnificent past.

The sunlight exposes the grime and dirt of the present day, the havoc overpopulation has wrecked upon the civic amenities. The sea of humanity staggers one's senses.

'*Adab, salaam ali kum.*' A grey-haired thin man in a weatherworn *kurta pyjama* greets them as soon as they disembark from their car. '*Huzoor*, I am the oldest guide around here. I can show you around and tell you secrets that you will not find written in any book. I will charge only two hundred rupees to show you around the Imambara in two hours. This will include the price of your tickets for entry into the Imambara as well. I shall tell you all about the history and the architecture of this place.' He speaks the last two sentences in English.

'Should we take a guide?' Pranjal asks Ruby.

'We should. This is our first time here. And neither of us knows much about the place.'

'Fine, you can start right away.'

'Sir, this is the Rumi Darwaza....' he starts.

'Pardon me for interrupting, but first may we know your name?' Ruby asks.

'I am Chand Ali.' He introduces himself. 'I will show you Lucknow in her greatest splendour. And you will fall in love with her.'

'I am sure we will, Chand*ji*.' Ruby looks at him and smiles. This tiny act of acknowledgement erases the worried frown from Chand*ji*'s brow and a little smile curves his stern mouth into a soft alignment.

'As I was saying, this is the Rumi Darwaza.' Chand Ali says indicating to the gate near which they are standing. 'It was built by Nawab Asaf-ud-Daula in 1784. Rumi Darwaza is inspired by a similar gateway in Istanbul. Hence, the name Rumi derived from Rome. It is sixty feet in height. During the days of the Nawabs, this place used to be aglow with beauty. On top of the Darwaza, a huge lantern lit up the structure at night. Come closer, you can see these artistically curved flower buds on the sides of the arch. Little jets of water used to rush out of each bud. This was then the gateway to paradise.'

'Wow!' Ruby and Pranjal exclaim in unison.

'Ugh, the response was in an awfully touristy style,' Pranjal says.

'Yeah, but conjuring the image in our mind has left us breathless—imagine how magnificent it must have been in the days that were,' Ruby responds.

'Come, now we shall enter paradise,' Chand Ali says. With a courteous bow he leads them into the gardens, mosques and Imambaras housed within the campus.

'You have to take off your shoes and leave them here. Mansoor, come here boy, give *huzoor* a coupon for their shoes.' Chand instructs, beckoning a young lad with a receipt book in hand. 'You may pay Mansoor two rupees for your shoes on your way out of the Bara Imambara. Now we shall see a modern architectural marvel built during the olden times. Please follow me. And... here it is.' Chand Ali presents with great flourish the residence of the Imam—a religious leader.

'This vaulted central hall is fifteen meters high and stretches fifty meters. It is said to be one of the longest halls in the world without any intermediary supporting pillars.' There is a quiet pride in Chand's voice.

'Impressive!' Pranjal murmurs.

'Awesome!' Ruby exclaims.

'Aha, now we shall see something even more amazing. Come let us climb up the stairs. The upper floor consists of labyrinthine passages—the *bhul-bhuliya*. Here I will challenge you to find your way out of the maze. Do you think you can find your way around?' Chand asks.

'Oh, this is way too confusing!' Ruby throws up her hands. The narrow passages form ideal ground for reverberation of any conversation. Suddenly the shrill sound of the screaming of a frightened child shatters the hauntingly mysterious atmosphere.

A couple have brought along their unwilling child inside. The poor child is hysterical with fear. His screams resonate along the narrow, dark passages, rising to a crescendo. Surrounded ominously by the nerve-shattering echo of the child's wails, Ruby refuses to go further. They make their way to the terrace upstairs, abandoning the frightened child dragged by a pair of most inconsiderate parents.

Ruby and Pranjal have discussed about having children. She adores babies and Pranjal wishes to become a Daddy when he still has the energy to play with them, run after them, and enjoy being a Daddy. They have agreed to start a family early. The quality Pranjal likes in Ruby most is her easygoing nature, her willingness to adapt to changes as fluidly as a river flows into an ocean—similarly growing infinitely with the change. Without shoving and pushing with the belligerence of a 'my feelings and me first' mind-set she still manages to smilingly sail through her life.

'How can parents be so insensitive to their own child's feelings?' Ruby shudders involuntarily. 'I wish we had some kind of a law to protect children from inconsiderate parents. Some parents can emotionally scare their children for life.'

If ever Pranjal needed substantiation in Ruby's aptitude in becoming a mother perceptive to their children's needs, he saw now that he had no reason to be anxious.

'Perhaps there is more pleasure in giving than in grabbing? Who knows?' Pranjal muses.

'I am the princess of the Arabian Nights and you are my prince.' Ruby declares as she prances around the patio pausing every once in a while to glance in wonder at the city below from a vantage position of the terrace. With domes and minarets dominating the skyline, the landscape does evoke the dreamy qualities of a fairy tale.

'This is stunning. Thank you Chand*ji* for showing us around so wonderfully. Do you live close by?' Ruby asks.

'Yes. You can see my house from here. Come,' Chand Ali says.

They look down below at the mess of hovels behind the palace. Huts made of discarded material, blackened by the sooth of pollution.

'That house in the corner with a clothesline is my home,' Chand Ali claims.

'And someone has washed your cloths very clean, Chand*ji,*' Ruby observes.

'That is my daughter, Noreen. She is a fine girl. She attends an English medium private school. I am illiterate. However, I have spared no effort to educate her. Her mother died when she was five years old. We are just the two of us at home. One day she will become a doctor,' Chand Ali says with pride.

'I'm sure she will make you proud, Chand*ji*.' Ruby nods sagely.

They sit there for some time. Chand Ali stands glancing at a distance with a vacant expression.

Ruby sighs as Pranjal softly murmurs the words:

How do you survive – the bitterness of the freezing night?
Where do you sleep – huddled in which secure corner?
In the graveyard, alongside the dead
Or
In the broken pavement – drawing warmth from the street cur?

Where do you hide your pain in this pitiless world?

How do you remain so noble a human in this era of mass duplicity?

O Celestial being, in your Earthly avatar?

At the gate as they bid goodbye to Chand Ali, Ruby offers a five hundred rupee note to him saying, 'For Noreen.'

They drive down to Ameena Bagh for lunch. 'Let's feast on *Nawabi* cuisine,' Pranjal suggests. 'You may have heard of their fantastic fare.'

'Interestingly, Lucknow style of *Dum Pukt* or maturing of a prepared dish, is said to have been born when Nawab Asaf-ud-Daula sampled the food cooked for the hundreds of workers engaged by him to build the Bara Imamabara, we have just visited. He built the Imambara to provide employment to people when famine struck Avadh.' Ruby recounts information as a local tour guide does.

'Yeah?' Pranjal is interested despite himself.

'Hmm... The food was cooked in huge vessels that were sealed on top and the dish was allowed to simmer in the slow heat of *bukhari* ovens. As the *handis* (huge pots) were opened, the delicate flavours delighted the Nawab.'

Their *dastarkhan*—meticulously laid out ceremonial dining spread include mutton *korma, nahari kulchas, warqi parathas* and platters of *kababs*. The finest mutton they have tasted in a long, long time.

That night they celebrate their Lucknow trip with a bottle of red wine. Ruby always speaks more candidly once she has had a few glasses of wine.

'Anita is in love with you.' It is a statement, not an accusation.

'She just thinks she is. I'm sure once she gets involved in a steady relationship, she will stop nagging me.'

'She hasn't been very successful in finding another guy. Perhaps we can fix her up with someone?'

'So that she gets off our back?'

'That. And it will be really nice to see her invest her affections wisely.'

'Invest her affections wisely indeed!' Pranjal drawls. 'I am glad we have transcended our passionate affair into an ecstatic dance of life together,' he declares.

'Yes Mr Poet,' Ruby grins. 'But we still need to guide Anita towards a more meaningful existence.'

'Yeah, tell me something I don't know, already,' Pranjal sighs.

'Things will change. You shall see,' Ruby promises, yawning.

Chapter 16

'Ram, Ram, *Taoji*.' Rajvir shouts his greetings and waves from his Mercedes Benz to his uncle who is driving a tractor. Rajvir purchases a new car every six months and finds it strange that Pranjal continues to drive an old model year after year. His uncle waves back with a smile. He is taking a fine-looking buffalo in the trailer of his vehicle. In Haryana, the buffalo is one of the most prized possessions and treated remarkably well.

Although fresh from his interaction with the Lucknowites courtly mannerism, the brash *Haryanvi* exchange no longer bothers Pranjal as it did earlier after his return to Gurgaon from his visits to Guwahati. In fact, he is pleasantly overwhelmed to discover that he has grown comfortable with their lifestyle without consciously making an effort. Just by being in the company of his friends, he has come to understand their way of life. In the same way, years ago he had learnt to understand and value the culture of the southern states after intermingling with friends from the region during his college days.

Rajvir and Pranjal are on their way to the site of the management institute which Rajvir is building in Rajpal's memory. These days buildings are sprouting faster than anthills in Gurgaon. Pranjal observes that every time he returns to this city from an extended tour, he perceives a new building where none existed before his departure.

Gurgaon is under frenzied development with its single-minded agenda of becoming a millennium city. It appears as if someone has brilliantly discovered that the barren moon is capable of supporting life and all the people in this populous country have descended upon the satellite to live the dream life.

They pass by the construction of the metro railway where workers seem to resemble little red ants in their fluorescent orange uniforms, busy creating a huge structure which will provide public transport to an ever-bulging population. There are similarly busy ants in Rajvir's building site as well, digging up hills and laying a solid foundation. Speedy structural erection is possible only when one has adequate money at one's disposal. In addition, Rajvir is clearly not cutting cost in establishing this institute in Rajpal's name.

Looking at the vast structure under way, Pranjal says, 'Rajpal must be looking down from the heaven above and personally thanking God for being blessed with a friend like you.'

'Dedicating this institute to his memory will keep alive our friendship,' Rajvir says.

Out of the blue, a troublesome thought niggles Pranjal. He recollects his stubborn refusal to contribute funds for constructing a *namgarh* in *Aita's* memory.

'A *namgarh*, in *Aita*'s memory? You must be joking. I haven't forgotten how she mistreated you, ignored my existence,' Pranjal said.

'I have. Why don't you? Bleed out the bitterness from your system, Pranjal, before the toxins poison your system,' Ma said.

'No.' Pranjal refused vehemently. 'Every time I think of her I shall remember how abominable people can be. Why should I contribute anything to preserve her memory? She never showed me the path to share, give or help.'

'I will not answer you that one. You will find out the answer in good time,' Ma never again raised the subject.

Pranjal notes that Ruby never allows the other person's meanness to come in her path of doing a good deed for that person. Her actions are influenced by her own judgement. He makes a mental note to send some money for the *namgarh*. With his ability to let go of the pain he had clung on to, the hurt that had held him bondage as a child, painlessly ebb away.

'Hey Pranjal, thanks for all that you are doing for Rakesh. I know Rajpal would have been mighty grateful to you for helping the boy turn a new leaf.' Rajvir interrupts his thoughts.

'He's doing fine. Ruby says that he is performing very well in Chennai. She rings him up every week.' Pranjal furnishes the information to Rajvir.

'Yeah. Yeah!' Rajvir nods, looking down at the gravel beneath his feet.

Pranjal senses his uneasiness, his difficulty in trying to dislodge his age old prejudice about a women's status. The hardest thing for him to acknowledge will be the fact that a woman is actually successful in accomplishing a feat where men have failed. His male prestige leads him to pretend that Pranjal is the person instrumental in reforming Rakesh rather than Ruby.

'He's a good guy. He can come and work here after completing his studies.' Pranjal subtly steers the conversation away from Ruby, mindful of Rajvir's discomfiture.

'Yeah, I hope he does. Rajpal was very fond of his nephew. It will give his soul peace to see that the boy is doing well.'

'Rakesh is more than doing well. He is doing excellent. The chap has not only taken up his studies seriously but is also growing up to be a well-balanced person,' Pranjal says. He wished he could add, 'Ruby has handled the situation with amazing maturity.'

There is a message from Anita in Pranjal's mobile.

'I love you.'

'That woman is an immature, self-centered creature. Marriage and commitment have no significance for her,' Pranjal mutters.

Anita's parents have been living separately since Anita was seven years old. They are very proud of their daughter's academic and professional achievements. Her mother had never been to school and her father never returned to her mother once he was posted far away from their village. In the city where he worked as a supervisor in a company, he remarried and lived without anyone from the village knowing about his acquisition of a new wife. It was only when Anita was in college she discovered his ugly secret.

However, both of her parents try their level best to keep their daughter happy. They ceaselessly try to make up for her unstable family life by fulfilling her demands and thoroughly pamper her as a child. Instead of growing up content with having all her wishes fulfilled, by a confused set of parents, her demands have just grown larger with age.

'You're frowning,' Rajvir observes. 'What is the matter?'

'A minor problem. It'll sort out of its own in due course.'

'Better to nib the problem in the bud than to let it fester.'

'It's a woman.' Pranjal needs to talk to someone about Anita.

Rajvir glares at him. '*Bhabi* is the most perfect bride. Anyone who thinks of cheating her will face divine punishment.'

'Relax, Rajvir. I know how lucky I am to have Ruby in my life. I shall never let her down. But it's this woman I studied with in college, who is now working with me in the office who is bugging the hell out of me.'

'Want me to teach her a lesson?' Rajvir asks gravely. Pranjal thoughtfully measures his instantaneous reaction and realises that he is deadly serious. It amazes him at the differences in their attitudes in solving a crisis. Rajvir assesses a problem instantly and speedily executes an action to eliminate the root cause of the trouble. Pranjal contemplates over the hitch weighing the pros and cons of every consequence before he takes an action. The consideration always remains how best to tackle a setback with minimum inconvenience to the concerned individual.

Rajvir's style of eliminating opposition is reminiscent of Rajpal's swift reaction. It sometimes amazes Pranjal how different he is in his outlook from these men who are his friends.

'Come on. Let's sit down in the car.' Rajvir looks at him strangely. 'Now tell me what is it that you really wish?'

'I guess I just want to run away from Anita's manipulative ways in the office. She is making it impossible for me to work in the office.'

'Then why don't you take leave and go on a short trip? You will be able to analyse the problem in a clearer perspective once you distance yourself from the situation. *Bhabi* deserves to be happy. The presence of this woman can only cause her pain.'

'No, Rajvir, she understands. She is the last person to let a woman like Anita affect her. Nevertheless, you are right. I need to get away for a few days to think clearly about the course of action I should take. We need to get away for a while.'

'Go to Jaipur. I have a house there. There is no one except the caretaker and the cook. You will be comfortable. You can stay there as long as you wish.'

'That sounds good. Thanks Rajvir.' Pranjal says and muses to himself, 'He is rather big-hearted.'

'*Areay bhai*, what are friends for?' Rajvir slaps Pranjal's shoulder. Pranjal is well aware of the fact that Rajvir is far more comfortable giving than receiving a favour.

That is how Ruby and Pranjal are out on a jaunt to Jaipur. As they drive past the NH-8 (National Highway-8), Pranjal can actually feel his tense muscles relax, his edgy mind compose a little, as he presses the accelerator.

'I never expected you to take off at such a short notice. You generally plan everything so meticulously,' Ruby smiles.

'Are you complaining?'

'I wish you would do it more often!' Ruby laughs and the wind steals the magical spell of her laughter into the never ending stretches of mustard fields; the millions of fiery golden flowers nodding their tiny heads with approval at her delight. Modern science and irrigation and the indomitable spirit of the Indian to work hard has transformed the once barren fields into yellow gold fields. Mustard oil is in great demand throughout the country these days.

January is a beautiful month to drive down to Jaipur. On either side as far as the eye can see, the mustard fields are in full bloom. The divider is abloom with burgundy bougainvilleas as the sun strikingly reflects their colour.

'They dress so colourfully. And such extraordinary mirror work.' Ruby comments as they cross village belles in colourful red *lehanga choli*. Their bright attires strike out vibrantly against the background of brown sandy landscape and jagged Aravalli hills of the countryside. The old Aravallis seems no longer to posses the powerful beauty of youth which the young Himalayas boldly display in so many other parts of the country. Yet they continue to survive and spectacularly enhance Rajasthan's splendour.

'I hope I never ever cease feeling small every time I look at the stunning grandeur of the world,' Ruby says fervently.

'I hope your eyes always dance dazzled with wonder, with the joy of living for the rest of our lives,' Pranjal wanted to say. He wanted to talk to her. Tell her all the things he had been hiding from her. He wanted to make a clean start without guilt and pain tearing his soul.

'Ruby…' He begins.

'Ooh, let's stop for a cup of tea in that restaurant.' Ruby points out to a bistro with tables invitingly arranged beneath umbrellas of bougainvilleas and honeysuckles to enjoy an alfresco meal while soaking in the winter sun.

They order tea and chocolate pastries. Exquisitely blended Assam and Darjeeling tea in fine silverware arrive to rejuvenate their spirits.

'Remember the time we were served milk in a separate glass, sugar in yet another tumbler and boiled red tea in a steel mug when I asked the waiter to serve us pot tea instead of boiled *chai*?' Pranjal grins at the memory.

'Such diversity. We don't even drink our tea in a similar manner. Yet, we have learned to live together in a country. Imagine Shyamlal Agarwall's family travelled all the way from Rajasthan to Assam in 1936 and settled there. You know Shyamlal's grandfather and my grandfather owned tea gardens in the same district.' Ruby says chattily as she drinks her tea.

Shyamlal is a rich businessperson in Guwahati. He owns hotels and restaurants across Assam. He is married to Ruby's second cousin. Pranjal had met him briefly and thought him a fine fellow.

'Shyamlal was a strict vegetarian before his marriage; now his wife, Pori, has become a staunch vegetarian and Shyamlal has turned a *pucca* non-vegetarian.'

'Love changes people's outlook about life,' Pranjal comments meditatively.

'Does it?' Ruby, smiling with her eyes, asks, 'Tell me how it has changed you?'

'I was a rotten liar, a scheming selfish swindler before you walked into my life and showed me the beauty of truthful existence. Had I been the man you have shaped me into, I would have fallen in love with you unconditionally without hatching plans to make you fall for me.' Pranjal fervently wishes he possessed the courage to voice his tormenting thoughts.

'I've always looked at the world through a rather narrow lens until I met you. It has forever been just my feelings and my mother's feelings I have been concentrating on.' He responds very seriously. 'Because I felt rejected by our relations during my childhood, I have never felt the desire to enquire about them. Yet I see you being equally nice to everyone even when you know people are maligning you. I am beginning to deduce that it is not such a bad idea to dispel this anger I have within me and just accept individuals for what they are, with all their limitations.'

'That's a very positive resolution, aspiring to look at the world in an unbiased manner.'

'I've got an excellent teacher.'

'But it is always more difficult to practice, you realise?'

'Of course I do. Nevertheless, I have become far more tolerant and flexible in my attitude than I was earlier. Like I no longer get as bugged as I used to when some nut honks like a lunatic if I take an extra second to start my car as the traffic light turns green. I let it pass without letting the bugger affect me.' Pranjal paused before adding. 'And I sent a cheque for *Aita*'s *namgarh* for the first time. I couldn't bring myself to be so generous earlier with all the tension within me.'

'That's commendable. And what about people you know? Are you as patient with them as you are towards strangers and relatives?' asks Ruby.

'I am patient with all I associate,' says Pranjal.

'Wow, really?'

'Really.'

'Really, really?'

'Of course!'

'What about Anita? Are you patient with her?'

'Anita?'

'Yes, Pranjal, Anita. Are you patient with her?'

'You of all people shouldn't be asking me to be more patient with Anita. You know she absolutely bugs the hell out of me.'

'But she loves you, Pranjal. You cannot expect her to outgrow overnight a love she has nurtured for years. She has loved you for years now. You need to give her time to outgrow that love.'

'She refuses to make an effort to look beyond what she considers is true love. She has become a nuisance.'

'Yet she was your friend once. You have moved on in life, but she is having difficulty letting you go out of her life. Perhaps you were the only steady relationship she ever had in her life. Maybe that is why she is so reluctant to let you go.'

'So, what am I supposed to do? Uncomplainingly suffer her advances and tolerate her folly until the time she decides to cure herself? Ruby, that woman is suffocating me with her irrational behaviour.'

'Okay, first and foremost, let's extricate ourselves from this demonical dictatorship of rationality. The point is as far as Anita is concerned, she is simply in love with you and she wants to be with you. There is no scope of struggling to be reasonable here now.'

'So what do you suggest? That I tag along with her method of madness?'

'Well, time is an amazing healer. She needs an adequate period and space to accept the fact that the man she loves truly loves another woman. It will take some time for her to come to terms with that realisation; but in due course she will learn to accept the truth.'

'While I patiently wait for her to come out of her mad infatuation, she goes around yapping to all and sundry at the office about our relationship which is but a figment of her imagination.'

'What are you afraid of Pranjal? I have no problem with her telling tales. Give the woman some time.'

'All those rumours will fuel tales of the office gossipmongers.'

'Let them gossip for a while. Even that will die down when they get no tittle-tattle to feed on.'

'How can you be so sure that all this will die down on its own without my doing something about it?'

'Because you have faith in yourself and you believe with your whole heart that this period of discomfort will soon end.'

'I believe!'

'Yes you do, Pranjal.'

'Fine, I will accept as truth what you say. It is easy to release myself from the mental bondage of Anita and her scheming behaviour. When I return to office, chances are, she will have conjured new ploys to pilfer my peace of mind but for now, I can sense a colossal burden of pressure ebb away from me.'

'How is Anita at her job, Pranjal? Does she take initiative in any specific departmental work?'

'Are you kidding? Initiative? That woman just comes to office and somehow manages to get her routine jobs completed. She spends the better part of the day playing office politics.'

'And she goes home to an empty house. Perhaps she needs a sense of belonging in her life. At the moment, she appears to be living a rather meaningless life. Her whole life is parcelled within the four walls of her office.'

'She does socialise, goes to the movies, pubs and hangs out with her friends.'

'Obviously there is still a deep vacuum in her life. At some point of time, she will wake up to the realisation that she is a victim of that painful fixation called unrequited love. You won't want to humiliate her when she comes to terms with her folly of obsessively loving someone who does not love her. However, for her to respect her ownself enough and refrain from demeaning herself by shamelessly continuing to chase you; she will first need to discover who she is and learn to first and foremost fall in love with her own identity.'

'Meaning? My darling Ruby, you do so easily cross over to the realm of philosophy within the course of a perfectly practical discussion that even the poet in me is baffled at times.' Pranjal opens his mind.

'She does not appear to hold her own person in high esteem. The trick is to love and respect the self so much that one will not allow it to stoop and grovel for another's affection. As of now she believes, her life will be complete only when she gets you. Now, she needs to understand that she requires filling that void within her with her own individuality. It needs to be instilled into her that another human being can only enrich us, not create our personality,' Ruby observes before continuing.

'Moreover, each one of us should have a goal worthy of striving for; of striding towards; to make our lives meaningful. Unfortunately, you are the objective she is struggling to obtain. Her life is an empty room and she is struggling to fill it up with borrowed furnishings.'

'What should she do?' Pranjal asks. 'Interesting metaphor.' He cannot help noting.

'She first needs to find a sense of purpose in her life; otherwise I am afraid she may sink into depression. At this moment of time, you happen to be the furniture she seeks to obtain. When she wakes and accepts that you are not available and admits that she cannot have you, she is bound to sink into a hole of dejection. Unless, of course, she already has an alternative goal worthy of pursuing, to occupy her senses.'

'And how does one find her a goal worth pursuing?'

'Pranjal, have you observed that we experience the most genuine satisfaction when we push our body or mind deliberately to its limits in an effort to accomplish something difficult and worthwhile?'

'I see what you mean. Like, strumming the guitar initially was a pleasant hobby. Stretching my limits to playing it better has now consumed me passionately. I am inspired to playing the guitar better the next day than I did the day before. This inspiration for perfection within me fills me with a desire to play the guitar everyday. In addition, I experienced a humbling feeling of gratitude the day I played with my friend John at a Church in Goa. It was a sublime experience to be able to share this gift with so many people that day and to bring joy to their hearts for those precious moments.'

'Precisely, each one of us should have a creative clutch to help us seek deep within ourselves to cherish the meaning of life. Ma, being wise guided you to develop a passion for a creative indulgence to enrich your life. Now a person like Anita has devoted her existence to getting an excellent score to gain admission in a good professional college. She has not harnessed any other talent she may have lying dormant within her. Unless she learns to search within herself for comfort, her coming to terms with your total lack of interest in her could prove to be harmful for her.'

'So?'

'Well, she doesn't like to go fishing, trekking, travelling, walking and doesn't play any musical instrument or sing; dance or read, paint or cook....she appears to have no other interest apart from you. We need to deliberate on what could hold her interest.'

'Tough job.'

'Actually it should not be such a though job. She enjoys socialising. I noticed she is good at networking. Why don't you talk to the Boss to put her in additional charge of the Public Relations Department? At least she will be interacting with a new set of people altogether.'

'That's a brilliant idea, actually. Why hadn't I thought of it myself?' All this while he had been trying to banish the issue of Anita as being a dilemma he has been caught in without looking at the situation from her perspective and then try to get to the bottom of her predicament as well.

'We all tend to look at a situation from the point of view we have conditioned ourselves to think. Take this tiny yellow flower. To a poet such as yourself, (Ruby winks) it is beauty in sublime gold. To a farmer it is a *rabi*, winter crop. To the botanist, the plant belongs to the genus *brassica*. From a nutritionist's point of view, ten grams of mustard seed contains 22.28 mg of magnesium, 38.92 mg of calcium and 1.88 gm of protein. For the conscientious homemaker, the loose, large and open plant along with the mustard flower is a useful vegetable as nearly all of the plant is edible. Each one of us is equipped with our own subjective outlook of viewing the world.' Ruby concludes.

'You definitely are blessed with the supreme sense of perceiving the world from an unbiased perspective. I certainly feel much better now that we have cleared the atmosphere of gloom surrounding the subject of Anita. I have a hunch that the Public Relations Department could bring about a positive transformation in her.'

'Good. Now enough talk of Anita. Let's enjoy our holiday!'

On their way to Jaipur, they see a mirage like settlement reminiscent of the Arabian Nights Tales with domes and minarets, a medley of Mughal and Rajasthani architecture.

'That is Amer. Pranjal, let's drive through the town. It looks like an enchanted land. You know, I read somewhere Amer was the capital before it was shifted to Jaipur around 1727.'

'Ah well the moon looks lustrous from a distance though she is filled with craters up close.' Ruby wrinkles her nose as a waft of sewage stink assault their olfactory senses. 'But imagine the grandeur of this place in the times gone by? There is a certain romance in the atmosphere of Rajasthan.'

'Are we falling in love with Rajasthan now?' Pranjal cannot stop himself from teasing her.

'No seriously. There are so many palaces, fortresses and citadels in this region and each site has a legend, a romantic tale associated with it. The Chittorgarh Fort, for instance, surely is one of the most romantic places on earth I can think of. Imagine the Sultan of Delhi, Alauddin Khilji was so smitten by the legendary beauty of Maharani Padmini Devi of Chittorgarh that he waged a war against Maharana Pratap Singh to win her. So many people died in vain. The Rani committed *jauhar*—burning herself along with all the other women to protect their honour.

'The Rajasthani women are renowned for their grace and beauty,' Ruby speaks with authority.

'And the men?' Pranjal enquires casually.

'Oh, the men are rugged and handsome. They have beautiful eyes, sharp nose and rich brown complexion. And they are pretty well-mannered too,' she grins.

'Really?' Pranjal asks struggling to maintain an impassive expression. He had never thought of himself as the jealous type. Now, he is not so sure.

'Really, except that personally I fancy the Eastern look.' Ruby winks at him mischievously.

Pranjal makes an effort to shake out of his mental stupor. How had he fallen in love so deeply with Ruby that he was actually experiencing a twinge of jealousy even at the thought of her finding some stranger attractive? He had started out pretending to be in love with her to lure her to serve his motives. When had the situation changed so drastically?

'Ruby, I have a confession to make.' He purposefully stops the car.

Ruby looks at him, assessing his tense countenance, his rigid body language.

'Confess only if you are still committing the bad deed; else, let it remain buried and dead. And you can rest assured I am not too into resurrection of the dead. There is enough in life to enjoy and be happy,' Ruby says.

'Are you sure? You may not feel the same once you know the truth,' Pranjal says.

'Do you wish to tell the truth? Do you feel it will make you feel better to get it off your chest?' Ruby asks.

'No,' Pranjal admits.

'Then forget it. Our experiences are valuable when they teach us to learn from our mistakes. If you have already learnt from your mistake and I can see that you are suffering from the pangs of repentance, then let go off the past and start afresh without any guilt. You do not have to confess everything to me, Pranjal. I told you earlier, I was quite aware that I was not marrying a perfect creation. However, I do expect you not to repeat the same mistakes,' Ruby says.

'I'll never let you down, Ruby. I want you to know that no matter what anyone tells you at any time or place that I will never let you down,' Pranjal promises.

'I trust you,' Ruby says.

Those simple words restored his confidence in their relationship. He realised no matter how hard Anita tried to complicate matters with the complexity of her way of thinking, she would never succeed in changing Ruby's mind.

This confidence inspired a liberating sense of daring within him to face the truth about himself. To admit the mistakes he had committed and bravely plunge on to correct them.

'You are bent on making an honest man of me, I can tell,' Pranjal smiles wearily.

So far, most of the good Pranjal did was for Ma. He did not wish to disappoint her. So he found excuses to explain his questionable actions. Anita's unrepentant deceptive attitude in its own way had cushioned his guilt. But Ruby's unquestionable trust in his honesty craved within him a desire to evolve his superficial self and elevate it to the level of his unspoiled inner being. His objective is to mould his metamorphosis into the man his mother had hoped that he would become.

Chapter 17

Pranjal wakes up in the middle of the night agitated by an inexplicable emotion. Ruby is sleeping like a baby. He looks at the clock. He looks at the clock—it is three a.m.' He gently covers Ruby with the quilt she had kicked off in her sleep, goes to the study, and switches on the light.

Something is wrong somewhere. Somebody, whose pain he can feel, is hurting tremendously. The streetlights are still on, illuminating the darkness outside. He waits for rosy-fingered Aurora, the Goddess of dawn, to flash across the sky in a saffron robe announcing the arrival of the Sun. His mind is blank as a white sheet of paper. The brass compass glimmers luminously in the brightly lit room to beckon his attention.

He logs on to his regular travel site via the internet connection in his laptop and books a ticket for Guwahati in the morning flight.

'Pranjal.' Ruby had walked in, her body soft from sleep, her hair tousled.

'Ma needs me. I can tell. I've booked a ticket for the nine a.m. flight to Guwahati. I'll let you know what exactly the matter is once I reach home. If all is well, I'll be back tomorrow morning.

In case, Ma needs us, I will let you know. You can take the afternoon flight.'

'Have you spoken to Ma?'

'No. Her phones are dead. Anyway, she is the last person on earth who will voice her problems. I need to see for myself there is nothing wrong with her.'

As Pranjal drives to the airport in the taxi, as he waits for the announcement of his flight, even as he sits waiting for the plane to take off, he keeps on trying her phones. The suspense makes him nervous. Her cell phone remains switched off and there is no response to the landline number either.

'God must be punishing me for all those times I avoided answering her calls, particularly when I was in the hostel. The apprehension of not knowing the whereabouts of her son must have caused her comparable anxiety. Please God, keep her safe,' Pranjal prays.

The windows are closed; the curtains are still not drawn, when he reaches home at one in the afternoon. His hand trembles as he presses the bell. Ma takes her time in answering the door.

She is ill. Pranjal has never before seen her bowed down with an ailment. She looks haggard and defeated. He hugs her.

'Pranjal, what are you doing here? Where is Ruby?'

'In Gurgaon.'

'Ring her up first. I'll put the kettle on.'

Hazy memories of a disturbed past suddenly appear crystal clear in Pranjal's mind. 'Close the door. Do you want the whole world to listen to our private conversation?' *Aita* would command Papa. *Aita* and her sons and daughters would be present in the room for family discussions, but Ma was never allowed inside.

Yes, Ma always takes care to make sure that Ruby forever feels secure and confident of being an integral and important part of the family. That she basked in the knowledge of being a most cherished member of the family unit.

Ruby must have kept her cell phone glued on her palm. She answers it as soon as he dials her number.

'Pranjal, is Ma all right?'

'She's fine, sweetheart. But as I am here, why don't you take the three o'clock flight and we can spend an extended weekend here.'

'That sounds good.'

'Right, I'll be at the airport by five thirty to pick you up. Take a taxi from the Yadav Taxi Service. I'll tell Raghu to arrange for your ticket.'

'Don't worry about the ticket. I've already booked it online. See you in the evening.'

Ma pours the tea into the cups. She butters slices of crisp, golden brown toast.

'You look like you haven't eaten anything since morning,' Ma says.

'You don't appear to have been looking after yourself either. Here, you have a slice of toast.'

'Is Ruby coming?'

'Yes, by the evening flight.'

'Your room is clean. I'll just have to put clean bed sheets.'

'Isn't Mita coming for work?'

'Oh, I gave her an off today. I wanted to sleep late.'

'Till afternoon?' I've never seen you lying in bed till noon. You are always up bright and early. You refused to remain in bed even when you were down with flu. What is the matter Ma?'

'I am growing old and senile.'

'You aren't even fifty, how can you be old and senile? And age never sat heavy on you.'

'Only an old lady allows forces beyond her control to pull her down because she lacks energy to carry on fighting.'

'What is to fight Ma?'

'My faith, I know I should not complain. I have the most wonderful son in the world and an angel of a daughter-in-law. But society sometimes delivers brutal blows.' When she gets this melodramatic, it invariably has something to do with the family.

'Kartik's marriage?' Kartik, Pranjal's cousin, is Ma's snooty elder sister's equally stuck up son.

'Imagine, practically the whole town has been invited to his marriage. Ketaki *baidow* asked me not to come over when I called her to enquire about the wedding preparations. She said it would be inauspicious to have me, a widow, attend Kartik's marriage.'

'She said that?' Pranjal exclaims. 'Such archaic traditional proclamation particularly coming from a woman who danced her nights away at the most happening clubs in town—that is rich. A woman who never abided by any custom, as far as I can recall. Perhaps she had decided to look up her history books to furnish a reason for not inviting us to the wedding.

'Ketaki has always been very proud of herself. But I never imagined the intensity of her meanness would make her sink so low.'

'We have lived with their prejudices all our lives, Ma. Why don't you come and live with Ruby and me for some time? The change will do you good and who knows you might even enjoy living with us.'

'You know how much I enjoy my freedom. I'm just feeling bad for being so humiliatingly ignored at this age. Not to worry, I imagine this pain too shall fade. Time always heals everything.' She sighs and pats Pranjal's shoulder. 'Thanks for coming Pranjal. Guess I needed your presence right now to reaffirm myself—worth.'

The three of them stay up late chatting. The following day is a Sunday. They drive down to North Guwahati early in the morning. The sleepy pace of this region is an idyllic location for the Krishna temple they have set out to visit. After prayers, they decide to go to the weekly *haat*—an open-air market at the Kachari *ghat* by the picturesque beauty of the Brahmaputra.

Vegetable sellers from the nearby villages come in ferries to sell their fresh vegetables and fruits in the market by the bank of the river. The market is a riot of colour. Further ahead is the fish market where fresh catch from the river is sold along with fish from the local fisheries.

The traders sell varieties of unpolished rice and preparations of rice like *aakhoi* (puffed rice), *hando guri* (roasted ground rice). Other household utility goods available in the market include cane products. *Dola*—a bamboo tray, used to separate the husk from the grains. The *dola* is held by both hands and flipped to toss the grain. As the grain in the *dola* swing up in the air, winnowing the husk midair, what falls back into the *dola* is the grain of rice. *Pati*—cane mats to lie down to enjoy its sleek, cool comfort on a humid, hot summer day. And pretty cane fans to carry along anywhere on a sultry day. Both Ma and Ruby adore this charming market.

As for Pranjal, he is rather well acquainted with a vendor from Arunachal Pradesh who stocks a good supply of *apong* (local drink) that he produces at home. Pranjal prefers this drink to any of the liquor available in the supermarkets and always picks up several bottles whenever he is in town.

After shopping, they have lunch at a restaurant overlooking the beautiful Brahmaputra.

In the evening they have a visitor. It is Ma's father, Pranjal's Grandfather.

'Good evening, Grandfather.' When had Pranjal started addressing him as Grandfather? It appeared as alien as he did at their doorstep. When was the last time Pranjal saw him visit them? Pranjal cannot recall. Addressing him in English, did Pranjal wish to maintain a formal distance with him?

'Hmm. You are looking good. How is Ruby?'

'She is fine. Come and meet her.'

'Aha, Kobita, I heard that you were not keeping well,' Grandfather addresses Ma.

'I am fine now. I was a little unwell. Nothing to worry about really. Must be old age.'

'Rubbish. I have yet to grow old. So it must be something disturbing you.'

'Nothing is disturbing me.'

'What about Kartik's marriage? Ketaki has invited practically the entire city for his marriage except you.'

'Well, it's her son's marriage and she is at liberty to invite whosoever she wishes.'

'But to ignore her sister for such an important function. I am ashamed of being her father at moments like this. It is our fault for spoiling her silly. All these women in the family have been treating you shabbily, including your mother. And the old fool that I am, I have been turning a blind eye to all their petty minded activities in order to maintain harmony. I realise now what a jerk I have been, letting Ketaki dictate every action in the family.'

'You have never wronged me…' Ma says.

'Maybe not, but I have not assertively tried to include you in the family particularly after Partho passed away. We have never been there besides you when you needed us. I watched your mother distance the family from you. I do not know why but your mother always felt intimidated by your presence. And that silly girl Ketaki, still hasn't learnt to handle sibling rivalry.'

That evening Pranjal learns many new things about his Grandfather. He learns that he wrote poetry as a young man; that he played the guitar and was part of a band during his college days; that he travelled across Europe for almost a year after graduation before settling down on a regular job. These revelations make Pranjal feel closer to his Grandfather.

None of them wanted that evening to end. Finally, Grandfather leaves well past midnight. Pranjal has never before seen Grandfather so relaxed and cheerful. A thought randomly crosses his mind. He reflects how lucky he is to have a woman like Ruby in his life, a friend who encourages him to better himself every day without ever laying any boundaries or restrictions. 'Thank you God, for creating her for me. Help me reciprocate her goodness every moment of my life.' Pranjal prays fervently.

All three of them end up attending Kartik's wedding. Their wedding invitation is delivered with due respect. Kartik's parents come over with the wedding card in a *horai*—a flat bell metal platter with an extended stand, on which are placed ripe orange hued *tamul* (areca nuts) and fresh green *pan* (betel leaves), prettily covered with a white coloured, delicate crocheted lace. This is the customary practice of invitation to an Assamese wedding. How does it matter that the invitation came on the day of the wedding? Ma is all too happy with the invite.

'How much easier it would be to simply let go. Ma does it. Ruby does it. Why can't I? What is it that is lacking in me that I cannot likewise discipline my mind? Why do I find it so hard to forgive *Deuta*?' Pranjal's thoughts stir his soul searching, even as he wears a cheerful face and participates in the festivities.

Chapter 18

In their emotional excitement over the marriage, they had missed out on visiting Ruby's parents. As a result, when they ring them the morning after the wedding, they are invited for lunch.

It appears the entire family has come to join them for lunch. Ruby's aunts, uncles, cousins and even a few neighbours are present drinking beer in the lawns. Trust Mrs Gohain to organize a 'little family get together' in style.

Pranjal notices that even that insufferably conceited fellow, Dhruva Bhuyan is present to grace the occasion. Dhruva is a promising politician son of a heavyweight politician father. He is one of the most eligible bachelors in the state. And everyone appears to be well acquainted with the fact that he has always been in love with Ruby.

'So young man, you have finally brought Ruby home, huh? You can't entirely steal her away from us Pranjal. You have not brought the girl home for over six months. Her poor parents have been missing her. I've never seen my sister so nervous.' Uncle Roop is referring to Ruby's Mom.

'Well one gets so busy. We were planning to come over for Bihu around the twelfth of April.' Pranjal is glad to be able to speak the truth. They had made plans to come home for the Bihu celebrations.

'Pranjal, there are just ten days left for the Bihu festival. Let Ruby stay back with us. When you come for Bihu, she will return with you.' Mrs Gohain says, joining them.

'Leave Ruby behind, and let that creep Dhruva hover around the vicinity? Besides, how am I supposed to live all alone in Gurgaon without her?' The very thought worries Pranjal.

'Yes, Pranjal, allow Ruby to stay back for a few days. We've all missed her terribly. And like Bhorokha says, it is only a matter of ten to fifteen days.' Mr Gohain has also gravitated toward Pranjal to second his wife's suggestion.

Pranjal returns to Gurgaon on Sunday morning. The apartment is a lonely place without Ruby. He orders Chinese from the outlet in the colony that provides home delivery services. He switches on the television and catches Liverpool and Chelsea in action. Football is the only sport that can arrest his attention at the moment.

By evening, he is restless. He decides to go down to the club to play pool. He meets a couple of colleagues and they hang around the club with a few drinks after the game.

'It's Fox's daughter's marriage tomorrow.' Keshav Sachdav says. Fox is their nickname for the head of Finance Department, one of the trickiest characters in their organization.

'I'm giving it a miss.' Pranjal is in no mood to attend weddings.

'Better go. Fox has a remarkable memory. He'll expect all of us to be present. And he does not know how to forgive,' Makhan Ahuja utters astutely.

'Well, like Daddy says, we've gotta give the Devil his due.' Ruby speaks sagaciously when Pranjal broaches the subject that night while speaking to her. 'Go and attend the wedding reception. Remember the old Assamese maxim, which says it is bad manners to ignore an invitation? The principle is that one should venture to the battlefield if one is invited but abstain from attending even a royal feast if one is uninvited.'

For once Pranjal wishes Ruby would digress from her correct ways and not suggest that he follow the right path.

Pranjal deliberately makes a late appearance with the purpose of getting the formality over with as quickly as possible. He is in no mood to socialise.

As soon as he steps into the reception arranged in the lawns of a hotel, Anita appears next to him like an apparition.

'Aha, look who has come minus the appendage of a wife tonight.' Anita moves as close to Pranjal as decency would allow.

'Hullo Anita. I am in a bit of a rush. I'll go ahead and wish the hosts.' Pranjal cannot wait to get away from her fast enough.

'Yeah run away, boy. But remember it's not me you're running away from. It's yourself; you're running away from, Pran.'

'Meaning?'

'Meaning you are afraid of your own reaction in my presence.'

'For Heaven's sake, Anita, we work in the same office. We meet almost every day.'

'But not like this.'

'Like what?'

'Like this.' Pranjal will never be able to fathom how she managed to pull it off in an area full of people but she let the *pallu* of her sari slip exposing her ample assets before nonchalantly covering them with the flimsy chiffon material.

'She expects me to be turned on, is it?' Pranjal fumes inwardly.

'Here, Chill.' He grabs a glass of electric blue coloured liquid the waiter has come forward to offer them and places the cold glass in her hand before marching forward resolutely to greet Fox.

'Good evening, Sir. Congratulations,' Pranjal shakes Fox's hand.

'Mr Handique, meet Sir Dhruva Bhuyan, a great personality from Assam.' Fox introduces Pranjal to the one person from Assam he does not wish to meet.

'Pranjal, pleasure to meet you again so soon.' Pranjal does not like his smile.

'You two know each other?' Fox is clearly pleased. Pranjal can almost hear the disc operating in his brain assessing ways on how to take good advantage of his acquaintance with this big shot politician to further his prospects of becoming the CEO of the Company. To attain that enviable position one needs every slug precisely shot with perfect astuteness in order to hit the bull's eye.

'Ah, yes we are family friends.' Dhruva heartily shakes Pranjal's hand. 'How are you doing, Pranjal? I don't see Ruby around?'

'She's in Guwahati. As *Bihu* is just around the corner she decided to stay back for a few days.' Pranjal hopes he does not grab the opportunity to run and visit her. 'I'll be joining her in a couple of days,' he adds.

'And in the meantime, enjoying your bachelor status, eh?' Dhruva winks at Pranjal as Anita joins them.

'Good evening Sir,' Anita greets the Fox.

'Good evening Anita. Meet Mr Bhuyan, a very important person. Anita here is looking after the Public Relations Department in our Company,' Fox introduces them.

'Delighted to meet you Anita.'

'I am sure he is.' Pranjal cannot help thinking. 'Bet he is busy calculating how best to influence her to cause mischief between Ruby and me. Little does he know that he has hit the jackpot if that is his motive?'

'Anita is looking after the Public Relations Department. You can get in touch with her in case you require any assistance.' Fox seals Pranjal's fate.

'Anita trying to get me back. Dhruva trying to win Ruby back. What a couple these two will make, hatching Machiavellian plots together.' The thought makes Pranjal sick in the stomach.

'Sir, a photograph, please.' The wedding photographer materializes almost magically at that inopportune moment.

'Yes, yes.' Fox of course desires a photograph with Dhruva. Dhruva of course wants Anita in the same frame with Pranjal. Hence, that faithful photograph happens. Anita slyly makes her way to stand beside Pranjal and lean toward him.

That is how that offensive much circulated photograph is taken. Dhurva photocopied a dozen copies from the printout Fox presented him. Ruby mentioned it to Pranjal that a copy slithered its way to her mother and another copy into Ma's hands.

'It's big news in the family, Pranjal. Dhruva has leaked the photograph to the local press. Today's supplement has the photograph with this misleading caption, 'Dhruva Bhuyan at a party in Delhi with an acquaintance from Assam, Pranjal with friend Anita. Also seen in the picture…' Pranjal, all my aunts and uncles are ringing up or have come home. Mom is in a tizzy. I know it must be Dhruva's monkey business, but how do I deal with Mom?' Ruby sounds worried.

Pranjal rings up Boss to brief him of his departure. He writes down a memo for an earned leave and places it on the Boss's desk .Then he takes the first flight to Guwahati. Well aware of the fact that if he gives Dhruva any more time, that chap will very cleverly poison Mrs Gohain's ears against him.

Pranjal heads straight for Ruby's home. He finds Ruby sitting in the cane swing in the lawn lost in a contemplative mood.

She is wearing a pastel coloured summer dress. She still looks cherubic. It strikes Pranjal that she never wears frocks and skirts in Gurgaon. There, she is always immaculately covered.

'Hi!' She looks up and smiles at him.

'Has she felt my presence?' Pranjal wonders. 'Her smile is dazzling sunshine; just to be in her presence is pure pleasure. I guess I'll never be able to survive without her. She has become the reason of my existence.' The revelation of his true feelings takes him unawares.

'Is it wrong to depend on another being for happiness? We search and look for happiness within us. We are doomed if we link our happiness with the existence of another individual. Dependence is dangerous. It can end in a catastrophe. What if I were ever to lose her? I would be devastated. I would die a thousand deaths of sorrow, grief and pain,' he ponders.

He continues to look at her loveliness and thinks, 'Then again, I would always have the illuminating beam of her love within me, comforting me through my darkest hour, forever illuminating my path. Her legacy of love will remain mine eternally. Nothing and no one can take that away from me. She is the personification of that sweet emotion of love that we are born to savour.'

'Hi!' His voice is a whisper as he breathes in the fragrance of her. They have been married well over two years and he is yet to get over the first flush of excitement he experiences every time he is close to her.

'I'm sure glad to see you. There is a massive family discussion on over the picture. It is unfortunate Dhruva met you in the same party Anita was in. Anita has obviously fed him with ample juicy tales about your so-called relationship. And he is wasting no time filling all my aunts, Mom and any relative who care to listen to him with all the cooked up details.'

'You don't believe him, do you?' They are at the doorstep.

'She is naïve, Pranjal. She is exceptionally innocent of the sly urbane lifestyle of a metro youth. Everyone advised me against marrying Ruby with someone working outside Assam. And now I have to rue it.' Mrs Gohain greets Pranjal at the doorstep.

'Borokha, where are your impeccable manners? Is that how we greet people these days?' Mr Gohain extends his hand and grips Pranjal's in a firm handshake. Pranjal prays this is a sign of reassurance. 'Come in Pranjal. I hope your presence will calm down all these charmingly agitated ladies of the family.'

'It is not a joking matter, *Bhindow* (brother-in-law),' Mrs Gohain's younger sister reproves sternly.

'Oh yeah, this is a family *panchayat* meeting. Ruby's aunts, uncles and cousins are all gathered discussing the great family scandal,' Pranjal groans silently.

'No it is not. So let us not make a mockery of the situation.' Mr Gohain asserts. 'Pranjal, come with me to the study. We can discuss this better in a peaceful atmosphere. Ruby, sweetheart, bring some tea for us in the study.'

Mr Gohain closes the heavy teakwood door. They sit down on the comfortable coffee coloured sofas by the window. Sunlight filters into the room through the white net curtains. The room resonates with the power and warmth of Mr Gohain.

'You must excuse my wife. I am afraid I have always pampered her. This is perhaps why she rarely thinks before speaking.'

He wanted to add that women needed regular reassurance about their worthiness and he constantly provided her with ongoing signs that she is loved and cherished.

Pranjal realises that although she is the same age as Ma, Ma never received such direct caring attention from *Deuta*. Thus, earlier Pranjal had incorrectly assumed that this difference in conduct was the outcome of a generation gap.

Now he understands that it is just a difference of behaviour between the two men. One man cared enough for his wife to reassure her frequently about her worth and another man held the opinion that a wife's feelings were of no great consequence.

'It is people like Mr Gohain whose positive actions steers in a catharsis in our society and creates a better world for the future generations to grow up in,' Pranjal contemplates.

'No, Sir, I can understand her agitation. Like any mother, she must be worried about her daughter. But I assure you Sir, this is all a misunderstanding,' Pranjal responds.

'I have no doubt that it is a mistake made by the papers, Pranjal. I know you can never do anything of which you would have to be ashamed. After all, you are Kobita's son.' His last sentence almost sounds like a proclamation pronouncing Pranjal the son of a famous saint. What standards has Ma laid precedence over for him to follow? Pranjal shudders at the thought.

There is a gentle knock at the door and Ruby walks in with a trolley laden with tea things.

'Ah, lovely. Ruby pour the tea, sweetheart. Here Pranjal, eat something. These tuna sandwiches are excellent. Nobody makes them better than Ruby,' Mr Gohain says offering a silver platter of delicately prepared sandwiches.

The rich aroma of classic Assam Flowery Orange Pekoe tea fills up Pranjal's senses, soothing him with its strong bouquet even before he has taken his first sip from the bone china cup with gold rim.

'I'll leave you two alone.' Ruby is gone in the flickering of an eye.

'Sir, I need to brief you with the particulars of the situation so that you have absolutely no doubt lingering about my conduct or my character. No Sir. Please let me complete what I wish to say.' Pranjal presents a verbal sketch for him in minute details, complete with facts he had even omitted telling his mother, for reasons he still fails to comprehend.

Perhaps it was the little boy in him trying to reach out to a father figure. Mr Gohain is a man; the closest Pranjal has come across who treats him like a son, as a corollary filling a void within Pranjal. Pranjal secretly missed having a father to steer him towards being a man. He needed Mr Gohain to understand him, approve of his actions.

Mr Gohain hears Pranjal out. He allows the younger man to speak without interrupting him even once. After he is done with his epic speech, he pours another cup of tea from the teapot.

'Here, have one more cup, son. You can use it.'

'Thank you.'

'My pleasure.' He smiles. And it strikes Pranjal that Ruby has inherited his smile. His smile is one of the most sublime smiles Pranjal has ever seen.

'You know Pranjal, it always amazes me, this discrepancy in our mind-set regarding friendship between the opposite sexes. The human mind is a most complex machine processing data obtained from all the sources the individual experiences and assimilates.' Mr Gohain pauses a moment before continuing.

'The female mind is even more complex as it absorbs information within a preconceived system assembled according to their personal prerequisites. Every perception transmitted by the female brain is a very special thought. I think the manner you have been handling the situation is totally commendable.'

He stands up and walks towards the windows. He stands looking at the colourful garden outside with his hands deep in his trouser pockets.

After a while he says, 'Pranjal, when I was working we used to have very private office rooms, very unlike the modern transparent glass chambers you have now. Although no one ever advised me, some sixth sense precautioned my mind and I felt the need to be on my guard at all times. I remember always leaving the door to my room ajar. It became an amusing subject of discussion among my colleagues. My friends poked fun at me when I insisted the secretaries leave the doors of my chamber ajar even when I summoned them to dictate memos. All the same, I stuck to my decision.

'By some strange quirk of fate, one of my good friends received his suspension order due to his misconduct with his secretary. He was never the bad sort but it is hard to think what goes on inside a closed door when someone comes out with damaging evidence. That is why it is always so important to be conscientious of our actions. Distancing from ones' accountability of the consequences of one's actions is like an enticing closed door. It can induce us to defy our ethics and prod us into acting totally out of character sometimes.'

'Dodging responsibility is a great human failing indeed,' Pranjal agrees.

'I won't condemn it quite so dramatically. Nevertheless, it certainly serves to premeditate the consequences of one's relationships, particularly those with members of the opposite sex. You take this precautionary measure because you value the other person enough as an individual to consider her mind-set as well. Personally, I feel the key to any relationship is maintaining a healthy space. The more impersonal you wish the relationship to remain, the more reserved should be your attitude.' Pranjal is not aware that Mr Gohain learnt these lessons from painful experience.

'I guess.'

'You can't be there at the beck and call of a friend and expect her not to be emotionally dependent on you. I realise you have remained a good friend to Anita. But her feelings towards you matured into love while yours remained stagnant in casual friendship.'

'I guess.'

'There isn't anything left for you to do Pranjal. The best course is to maintain a respectable distance from her. Until she wakes up to the reality minimise your interactions to a totally professional level. It is not enough to say you are disinterested in her, watch out to confirm that your body language is not telling another story. Another essential point is to desist from inviting her to your parties and social dos. I know Ruby with her gentle nature will insist on handling her with kid gloves. *But you will need to take a tough stance son.'*

'Yes, Sir.'

'Start focussing on cementing your relationship with Ruby. Remember, even a brilliant woman like her needs to be singled out and treated specially. Both of you are lucky to have a solid foundation because of your similar ideological upbringing. Devote your energies in growing into your fullest potential instead of wasting time on Anita.'

'But she'll still be present in the office trying to cause trouble.'

'The exquisiteness of total concentration is that you will automatically tend to overlook her presence even when she is physically in the room. When we consciously decide to eliminate a particular individual from our orbit by refusing to acknowledge their presence, we mechanically cease to be aware of their existence. They become part of the scenery of perfect strangers who cross our paths every day but whose countenance we fail to register in our memory. Remember no woman likes to be ignored. Be assured she will return the compliment pretty soon.'

'You have inspired confidence in me, Sir. Guess I needed some authority to motivate me to take such a monstrously drastic step. I've never been rude to anyone before.'

'That I can understand, being brought up by Kobita single-handedly.' He laughs. 'She probably drilled it well and good into your mind never to be rude to anybody. Kobita and Ruby are similar in their sensitive outlook of life. But one needs to take a tough stand when the situation demands.'

'Well I guess I can give it a shot.'

'Good. Remember, never compromise on your values. In addition, do not worry too much about your job. You are an intelligent chap. There are dozens of options always open for you. Now I think we should go out. The suspense must be killing Borokha,' Mr Gohain grins.

'Thank you, Sir.'

Mr Gohain smiles and puts his arm on Pranjal's shoulder as they make their way out of the room.

Chapter 19

Without informing Pranjal, Ruby arranges to meet Anita for a coffee.

'So, Pranjal's wife, tell me what is it you want from me?' Anita asks mockingly as she makes herself comfortable.

'Nothing,' Ruby replies. 'I want nothing from you. I just thought we could perhaps have a talk, get to know one another.'

'Come, come. You haven't invited me to share a coffee merely to enjoy my company. You have come with the agenda to talk me into leaving Pranjal alone.' Anita has certainly perfected the art of smirking. 'Pranjal, who can make me feel worthwhile, happy and complete.'

'A partner cannot make you feel worthwhile, happy and complete unless you are capable of feeling them about yourself first.' Ruby responds. 'No one else has the power to give you what you are looking for.'

'Pranjal can give me every reason to be happy,' Anita declares Passionately.

'Can he, Anita? Do you really think you can be happy with a man whose ideology has so diverted from your perception of life?'

'I believe what he believes,' Anita states. 'Whatever he thinks, says, does is right as far as I am concerned. I am always willing to change my likes and dislikes to his likes and dislikes.'

'Perhaps you shouldn't undermine the importance of your personal likes and dislikes merely to fall into line with that of another individual. You will only be strangulating life out of your uniqueness,' Ruby says.

'Why don't you wake up to the truth?' Anita snaps. 'Pranjal married you because of your family background. You two have nothing in common. A marriage cannot survive when the partners are so different.'

'Pranjal has changed since marriage,' Ruby says.

'You think Pranjal has changed into some boring guy who no longer relishes the thrill of power and achievements? If you are under the illusion that a person can change so much, you are living in a fool's paradise, my dear. Mark my words, Pranjal will soon be bored with you,' Anita says.

'I cannot predict the future, Anita. But perhaps Pranjal is already bored of you?' Ruby retorts.

'You little two bit writer! Oh, you think you are smart, do you? Well, sorry to pour cold water over all your well-laid plans. But I will never stop loving and trying to win back Pranjal,' Anita states. 'Wake up to reality, madam dreamer.' Anita gets up and almost knocks down her chair in her haste and agitation.

"Never' is a very long word. So long that even our memories fail us in trying to recollect it at times,' Ruby says. 'This is a good thing because we can live a meaningful existence only when we continue to stride ahead in our search of ourselves. And leave the past behind.'

'Do you really think you can fool me with your charade of trying to project yourself as some kind of a perfect woman?' Anita speaks over her shoulder as she makes her exit. 'It is to cover your drab ordinariness, your unquestionable plain looks and doubtful intelligence. You have perfected the art of projecting yourself as a good human being because that is the only recourse left for you to squeeze a foothold for yourself in society. You are nothing but a loser. I feel sorry for you. But you will lose Pranjal soon. Start accepting that, madam.'

Ruby watches Anita walk away. She offers a quick prayer for her.

Chapter 20

On his return to office, Pranjal receives a rude shock. His transfer letter awaits him on his desk. He is instructed to report to Patna Office, at the earliest date. Pranjal has no issues with a Patna or a Shrinagar posting. After all, he is from the North East. A posting in the so-called troubled zones does not alarm him.

However, to be this unceremoniously removed out of his seat infuriated him. When he requested Boss Perfect to grant him a day off to visit Guwahati to solve a personal problem, his boss had encouraged him to go. Pranjal left for Guwahati on Friday and returned with Ruby to Gurgaon on Sunday. They gave the annual family celebrations of *Bihu* festival a miss to avoid applying for additional leave. Monday morning, Pranjal finds this slip of paper, destroying his faith in another officer. Boss Perfect was the last person he had expected to take such a low down step.

Being transferred and downgraded adds insult to Pranjal's injury.

Pranjal had joined the Delhi office with great expectations; opting for a posting in the capital city because he felt Delhi offered a forward-thinking milieu for him. Delhi being the capital of the country and not that of any particular state is a melting pot of all the different states. This is one big metropolis where individuals from every state of the country can equally expect to feel at home.

Pranjal looks once more at the letter: Shri Pranjal K Handique, you are hereby released from duty with effect from 05-04-08 and intimated to join the Patna office latest by nine a.m., 07-04-08. The offending note was signed by Mr T. Dwevedi, Personnel Department.

Pranjal cannot remember ever writing such a brutal transfer note during his tenure in the Department.

Pranjal rings Ruby to break the news.

'But that's unethical. How can you be transferred without assigning a valid reason?'

'They have a reason. I am needed in Patna office, the letter states.'

'That is a blatant lie. That small office in Patna barely has four persons. There is no scope for posting a midlevel officer there. A much junior person has always been in charge.' Ruby knew all about the Patna office because they had dropped by at the office when they visited Bihar for the travel pieces she was working on in Nalanda and Bodh Gaya.

'Aaa ha, but the management now feels there is requirement of a mid level officer.'

'A doctored lie. You are performing excellently. Moreover, your service is required here. You have done no wrong. No, Boss can transfer you according to his whims and fancies. It is not a private company.' Pranjal can picture Ruby making a face. She screws up her mouth and nose when she gets agitated. She chews her lips when she tries to resolve a crisis. She makes optimum use of all her energies in her effort to solve a problem at the earliest.

Plainly, she has no patience when it comes to being stuck with a predicament.

'We can't let them get away with such injustice. Clearly, Anita is instrumental in influencing the Boss's decision. We have no problems with the transfer. But we have to prove them that we are not pushovers to be messed with just because we are honest and hardworking and refuse to join the bandwagon of office politics.'

'I know.'

'Talk it out with Boss Perfect. I am confident he will see reason and act impartially once you explain the situation clearly to him.'

'Let me try.' As soon as Pranjal switches off his cell phone, Anita appears.

'Hi, Pran. So sorry to hear about your transfer. It's going to be such an inconvenience for you and Ruby. Do let me know if there is any way I can help,' Anita smirks.

Pranjal ignores her and walks to the Boss's chamber. His secretary allows Pranjal in.

'Morning, Handique. How are you doing? Everything settled at home?' Boss Perfect is sweet.

'More than settled Sir. Thank you.'

'Do sit down Handique.'

'Thank you, Sir.'

'The management urgently requires your services in Patna. That is why we have decided to release you at the earliest.'

'Pardon me Sir. But Sir, what beneficial outcome will come out of this shuffle at this juncture to the Company, Sir?'

'Are you questioning my management ability, young man?'

'No Sir, of course not. I would never be so impudent. I am simply trying to comprehend the rationale behind my going to Patna and working in an office where there are no officers except a supervisor and an assistant. I wonder what my duties will be in such an establishment.'

'The necessity has arisen, hence the transfer. You will be briefed on the nature of your duties as soon as you reach there. Ahuja will get in touch with you. I am afraid we shall have to end our discussion. I am extremely busy at the moment.' Boss dismisses him. He fusses over impatiently with his cell phone, calls his secretary on the intercom and looks with deep concentration at the papers on his desk.

'So he wants to act the Big Boss and show what a small fry I am in this organization by wilfully playing out his fancy,' Pranjal fumes.

'Sir, do you have any complaint against my performance that you so wish to literally demote me by asking me to report to Ahuja knowing very well that we belong to the same batch and are of equal rank?'

'I need a more dynamic person here in the corporate office. Things move very fast here, you know. Handique, no offence, but you are more suited to the slow pace of a site office.'

'Even though all the work gets gone fastest in my department?'

'Mr Handique, I am not arguing that your performance is good.'

'It was outstanding, last week, Sir. You said I was outstanding last week.'

'Well, I still stand by the fact that you are an efficient, honest, diligent worker.'

'Thank you Sir.' Pranjal goes home. Ruby is not at home. He locks himself in the study. His mind is a complete blank.

Without giving himself time to contemplate over his actions, he dials the Gohains' number.

Mrs Gohain answers the phone. 'Pranjal, what a pleasant surprise! How are you dear?'

'I am fine, Mama. Thank you. Actually, I am in a terrible mess.' Pranjal needs to solve his problem desperately. And he spills all to the first sympathetic ear ready to hear him out.

Just then, Ruby walks into the house and activates the parallel cordless receiver to make a call. Her mother's voice at the other end of the line stumps her. When she hears Pranjal's response, she is about to switch off the phone.

At that precise moment she hears her mother say, 'Don't tell any of this to Ruby, Pranjal. You know how simple she is. Now Pearl would have been an ideal wife for you. She would have known how to deal with these situations. She is so perfect in managing people. But our Ruby is far too committed to her idealistic principles. You and I both know that the world does not run so smoothly. We need to twist and turn people's concepts to mould them into our way of thinking.'

'How do I change my Boss's stance?' Pranjal asks.

'Don't you worry, you poor boy. I will speak to Gautam just now and ask him to have a word with your boss. What was his name again? Right. You can go and meet the man in the afternoon and see the change in him.'

'Thank you so much. I don't know what I would have done without your help. I was totally freaked out and didn't know whom to turn to,' Pranjal gushes.

'We should keep in touch, dear. I am always there to help you. The next time you are in Guwahati, spend some time with Pearl. You are family now. She will be able to give you valuable tips. She is an extremely intelligent and smart woman.' Mrs Gohain continues. 'And remember, there is no need for you to speak about everything to Ruby. What you do outside your home is your business alone. What she does not know cannot hurt her. After all she is your wife, not your confession box!'

'Yes Mama.'

Ruby does not prolong her agony by listening any longer to their conversation. It does not take great wisdom to conclude that Mama is trying to expose Pranjal's weakness to the family.

Ruby had always clashed with her mother on the fundamental principles of living.

'You have to be practical Ruby. Marry Dhruva. He is rich. You will have a comfortable life and never lack anything,' Mrs Gohain insisted.

'I cannot marry Dhruva merely because he is rich. That would be wrong,' Ruby refused.

'You are a stubborn girl who refuses to look beyond that proud little nose of hers. The day is not far away when you will bitterly regret not listening to me,' Mrs Gohain stated.

When Pranjal proposed with the words, 'I've never before met a girl I wished to marry. You are as principled as my own mother is. I can't think how I got so lucky to have met you.' Ruby gullibly believed him. She was desperate to break free from her mother's domineering presence in her life.

The conversation between Pranjal and her mother she had unintentionally overheard dazed her. How could he strike a deal with her mother to enlist Uncle Gautam's help to maintain his position at the office?

Ruby admired Pranjal of being a self-made man. She was shrewd enough to have an inkling about the compromises he must have made to establish himself without anyone to lend a helping hand.

What she never imagined was that Pranjal's idealism was a farce, carefully contrived purely to win her over.

Ruby realises she needs space to find answers to the questions which are creating an unbearable cacophony in her mind. She cannot face Pranjal in this disturbed state. She waits in the guestroom until he returns to his office before taking a decision. Scribbling a hasty note to Pranjal, she dashes for the airport.

Much later, in the welcoming comfort of Ma's sitting room, Ruby hugs herself tightly with her arms, her legs curled up, looking vulnerably alone in the big sofa.

'I figure I had a mental picture of the qualities I wished for in a husband. I didn't want him to fulfil all my needs and aspirations and be the foundation of all my happiness for my entire life. All I ever wanted was for a man to love me for whom I am as a person rather than love me only for being a part of the family.' Ruby speaks contemplatively. 'You know, my feeling is that the individual 'I' should shine through enough to attract the man. Rather than the package being the irresistible temptation and the 'I' lost in obscurity within the dazzling package.'

'And Pranjal appeared to meet all the must haves in an eligible husband,' Ma sighs.

'The sad part is that he should betray me on the very subject I feel so strongly against.'

'That is why he chose not to tell you,' Ma says.

'But isn't consulting one another in important professional and personal decisions laying the foundation of a solid marriage?' Ruby asks. 'One lie can destroy so many years.'

'I agree it was wrong of Borokha to encourage Pranjal to refrain from discussing professional and personal matters with you. Even worse was her suggestion that Pranjal turn to Pearl or her instead. But we both know Borokha's nature. No one can change her,' Ma says.

'It's not mother I am angry with. She laid down her rules long ago. But I am hurt because the one person I had thought would never lie to me failed me so callously,' Ruby says.

'Pranjal has a lot of explaining to do before I let him venture anywhere near you. Not informing you about his equations with his friends, colleagues, relations are disregarding your marital vows where you promised to be true to one another and I would say it is tantamount to emotional abuse.' Ma takes a deep breath. 'Borokha will continue to think of new ways to retain her control over you. But if Pranjal does not have the courage to make his own decisions and fails to fulfill his commitments towards you, trust me even though he is my only son, I will not hesitate to disown him.'

Ma walks up to sit beside Ruby and gives her a hug.

'Thank you for being so good to me, Ma.' Ruby sniffles tearfully. 'Thank you.'

Chapter 21

'Look, Pranjal, you and I go back a long time,' Boss says. He calls Pranjal to his chamber the moment Pranjal returns to the office in the afternoon. He is his old, very affable self again. Pranjal is left wondering whether he had really seen the other side of the Boss.

'Sure, we went back a long time. I am the one who helped in moving your promotion file to the Prime Minister's Office by requesting my childhood friend Prasenjeet, now a member of Parliament, to help.' Pranjal thought vindictively. Technically, Boss owed him a major credit for helping him attain his present position.

'This woman, Anita, is a monumental nuisance. I am tired of her whining ways. I cannot afford to transfer her to another region. She is bound to cry foul play.' Boss is in a quandary.

'You could relocate her to a different office.' Pranjal suggests coolly. 'The Training Institute. It's in a different locality in the city.'

Anita will wreck vengeance for transferring her to the Training Institute. However, for the Boss at this instant, her wrath is not more perilous than Pranjal's discontent. Pranjal's ace is far more powerful. Gautam can obliterate all his plans of ever becoming the CEO.

'Of course, Handique, We will sort it out. After all, your promotion is due next year.' Boss is almost fawning yet he is cunning enough to remind Pranjal of his forthcoming promotion.

'And this, Sir?' Pranjal asks innocently holding up his transfer letter.

'Forget about this scrap of paper. Consider it never written.' He takes the now useless sheet from Pranjal's hand and crumbles it viciously before throwing it into the waste paper bin.

Boss Perfect has only one true love and that is his career. Everything else is momentary distraction. That is why he wastes no time in ruthlessly clearing the path to fulfil his ambition.

To carry on in this competitive arena, Pranjal has learnt to raise his fangs as well to preserve his position.

Pranjal returns to his seat and broods over what had just transpired this morning. What is it Ma had said, 'Life is meaningless unless you make personal commitments to give it meaning.' By being a manipulative strategist, Pranjal was following the set of principles laid down by his professional predecessors. However, his action went against the essence of his nature. He is not proud of what he has just done.

That evening he decides to leave his car in the basement parking lot in the office and opts to travel by public transport. He boards a city bus and lets his mind wander. He has not travelled in a city bus since college. Somehow, travelling by bus makes him feel young and relaxed. Perhaps, because the experience is reminiscent of times when he was a carefree student; perhaps, because he feels clad in anonymity in a bus crammed with strangers; the ride permits him to sink into sagacious contemplation.

He looks out at the charming scenery of Delhi from the window. As a college student, while commuting by the recklessly driven city buses, he had promised himself that he would earn the very best of everything life had to offer. Swanky cars, a beautiful home, a hefty bank balance, holidays abroad and a cushy job.

He was doing pretty well for himself so far. Until this morning. There is this voice inside him. Ma always told him to listen to in the silence. However, when it had strained its limit to make itself audible, Pranjal habitually switched on the music loud or drank with his friends until the voice faded away.

The voice is trying to communicate with him now. Amidst the chatter within the bus, Pranjal finds himself straining to sooth his muddled mind in a cocoon of silence. The words around him fade and his surroundings blur out of existence as all his concentration become engrossed in deciphering the voice within.

'Am I wavering from my search for the true personal meaning of life? Am I losing the essence of myself in the pursuit of my happiness? Can I remain happy without being able to face myself when I communicate with my inner voice? My inner voice tells me I am perhaps not altogether right in my understanding of happiness. Lawfully, I have committed no crime. Morally, I have not sinned. Nonetheless, I am deeply aware that I had not acted in the virtuous manner I wished to conduct my life.' Thoughts, which have strived to resurface repeatedly, deluge his mind.

By dropping Gautam's name, he fulfilled his immediate goal to subdue the menace of the Boss. Nonetheless, he is unhappy.

'In your enthusiastic endeavour to treasure that unwavering and enduring trait termed happiness, always remember to thread with caution. Be careful to avoid falling into the pit of indulgence and instant gratification of senses,' Ma had cautioned him.

'What is happiness, Ma?' Pranjal was a testosterone pumped teenager trying to mull over the meaning of his existence in a world filled with children of his age who appeared to have everything because they were so rich. Pranjal was close to tears that day since at the playground, Kartik, his cousin mockingly introduced him as his poor cousin to the pretty girl who was new in their neighbourhood.

Ma had said, 'Pranjal, quickly smile and wash away that frown. Multiply your happiness Pronto.' Pranjal had then questioned the meaning of happiness.

'Sweetheart, this sensation you are experiencing right now is a momentary mood. We can soon make it disappear by rationalising our thoughts. Happiness is a *profound* experience achieved through a meaningful life by exercising your *immense* strengths in a purpose *greater* than your own immediate goals.' Ma emphasised words for effect when Pranjal was young.

'That's some philosophy, Ma.' Most of it had gone over Pranjal.

'Aim to be everlastingly happy, Pranjal. There is a little voice locked up inside all of us, which guides us to thread the correct path. We have to listen to that voice very deeply, in silence, with great concentration.'

'When we abide by this voice, we remain happy always. Happiness is a most precious gift; cherish it every moment of your existence to enrich the meaning of your life. Don't fall into the trap for seeking instant gratification of the senses.'

She knew that some day Pranjal would comprehend the meaning of her words. She smiled and they spent the rest of the afternoon drinking hot chocolate and talking late into the evening. They were happy and content.

After all these years, her words resonate their meaning in his life. Pranjal cannot abandon his integrity and stoop down to win because he cannot act against the principles ingrained in the person he has grown into.

'I cannot sacrifice my happiness merely to settle scores for short-term excess. I need a backup plan to lead a more fulfilling life,' Pranjal thinks.

In the past, Pranjal had been blasé about brushing aside Ma's teachings. Since his marriage, he has unconsciously evolved into an individual Ma would be proud to introduce as her son. Every moment of every day, through words, through actions, she had patiently pointed out to him the path to happiness.

When he returns home to unload his weight of mental agony he finds Ruby's note conspicuously stuck on the television screen in the drawing room. It is too late for him to catch a flight to Guwahati that day. It is too early for him to spend the night tossing in an empty bed.

The apartment, with its stable aura of positive vibrations emanating from every corner suffocates him in his own disturbed presence. Ruby had liberated him from his self-centred world where amassing money was his sole agenda in life. As a man blinded in an accident, who is once again able to see the world; Pranjal now perceives the multidimensional experience that is life.

He walks out of home and heads for the pub he had frequented as a bachelor. As he sits brooding over his drink, Anita gilds along in a slinky dress and seeing him makes her way towards him. She sits herself on the empty chair in his table without bothering to ask acquiescence. She crosses sheer stocking sheathed legs with great deliberation as she sits down.

He observes her wordlessly.

'Ruby has left you, hasn't she?' Anita gives her annoying smile. 'It was bound to happen. You two are poles apart. For her, marriage is some sort of an idealistic sacred commitment where two people are to remain ever faithful, honest and blah, blah, blah to one another. We two are too sophisticated for that kind of regressive mindset, Pran darling.'

'She hasn't left me. She has just gone to be with Ma for a few days.'

He did not tell her that Ruby had switched off her cell phone and refused to take his calls. When he had informed Ma of his intention of flying to Guwahati, she had counselled him against such a rash act. She suggested that he give himself and Ruby some time to arrive at a decision.

'What decision, Ma? I need Ruby in my life!' Pranjal exclaimed, exasperated at her suggesion.

'May I remind you that a marriage is not merely about gratifying a single individual's needs, Pranjal? Both partners should evolve to greater echelon through the alliance. What on earth lead you to assume that the institution is some form of contractual slavery?' Ma sounded angry.

'Ma, I've hardly treated Ruby like a slave!' Pranjal exclaimed. 'That's a bit farfetched statement. Don't you think?'

'You may not have physically mistreated her. But I have observed that the poor girl has been the one constantly making the adjustments. First, it was the matter of Anita and now this abominable act of lying to her. You, of all people should know where this kind of behaviour of yours will lead to.'

'First, Anita!' Pranjal mulled over Ma's accusations. She had never accused him before.

Pranjal looks at Anita. Anita's luscious honey hued complexion lends extra delectability to her sensuously voluptuous figure. Even when she walks, not just her limbs, but her entire structure appears to glide in a sensuous tale. There is a dangerous restlessness about her that is disturbingly attractive, even when she is apparently simply sitting quietly.

In sharp contrast, Ruby's calm personality emanates an aura around which serenity appears as an eternal companion.

Pranjal had so far successfully suppressed his simmering conflicting emotions and restrained himself from waddling in his wayward ways. However, the shock of coming back home and not finding Ruby had shaken him out of his oblivion. He had to make a choice. Ruby's action firmly laid down the ultimatum.

He could still hook up with Anita and continue with the lifestyle he was living. Anita had no issues. She loved him unconditionally. He did not need to wed honesty to marry Anita.

On the other hand, Ruby's love for him did not embrace his deceptive and dishonest nature or his dual contradictory philosophies in life. Her love would not accept him as a liar but would expect him to reform.

He would have to make a choice as to how and with whom he wished to spend the rest of his life finally.

'I am going to have it all, one day. Money, status and fame.' Pranjal always started his conversation with this same sentence during his college years as if by repeating the line he would will the words to take concrete steps.

Now, the very foundation he had built his life on threatened to destroy his happiness. The realisation hit him like a physical blow at his core his whole world was meaningless without Ruby beside him.

'What are you thinking so hard?' Anita deliberately introduces huskiness in her voice. 'Thinking too much complicates life. Sail with the flow.'

'That's the idea,' Pranjal says. 'I've all my life deliberated over my actions to ensure maximum profit. That is going to stop now.

I am going to drop that baggage and start afresh. Bye Anita. Take care of yourself.'

'Where are you going? You cannot go after Ruby. When I said, go with the flow I meant embrace what we have here. We can be happy together Pran.'

'My happiness lies with Ruby, Anita. I am sorry.'

Anita watches him walk out on her yet again. Her tragic flaw had always been her inability to accept Pranjal's unrequited love. She tried to win him through fair and foul means. But as he walks away she feels a door slam at her heart. Her heart hurts as if a heavy iron lock has permanently closed the door to life.

Pranjal reaches Guwahati the following day.

'I thought I asked you to wait a few days and clear your thoughts before you came,' Ma greets him.

'I need to speak to Ruby, Ma. She is a part of my life.'

'Very poetically correct, my son. But I don't want you causing the girl any more pain. Heaven knows, she has had a hard enough life suffering silently her mother's idiosyncrasies without having to confine the rest of her life adjusting to your selfish nature.' Ma pauses just long enough to catch her breath. 'I completely fail to fathom how any child of mine could use another human being as callously as a stepping stone to fulfil his detestable greed.'

'I made a mistake. Ma, at least I am honest enough to admit that,' Pranjal says.

'You have come back because you do not want to lose Ruby and all that a marriage with her entails you to,' Ma says. 'Being a part of her family is what you in fact desire.'

'I've come back because I have realised that I cannot live without Ruby. My success is meaningless without Ruby by my side to share it with me.'

'If you lie and cheat her, how do you expect her to be by your side?' Ma asks.

'I promise never to lie ever again to her. Ma, I was wrong to think that fulfilling my ambition was all I ever needed to be happy. I've never felt so lonely and hollow inside.'

'Marriage, this commitment you have made with Ruby, is a living organism where the focus should ideally shift from 'I' to 'we'. If one partner violates the dignity of the other partner, then this relationship can shatter. If you are planning to hide, lie and keep secrets in your marriage, let me assure you that your relationship will wither away. Without complete trust and respect on both sides, marriage is a meaningless, hollow, social obligation. I lived making compromises because my expectations from my marriage included a family and a home. That was all. Ruby on the other hand, choose you as her life partner because she believed you to be ethically empowered enough to be sensitive to her feelings, as she is to yours.'

'I am sorry,' Pranjal says.

'Being sorry is not enough. If you are going to hatch surreptitious plots with other people and leave Ruby in darkness of your secret agenda, you do not deserve her. When you refuse to reveal your true feelings to one another, the relationship cannot bloom,' Ma says. 'But then you are a man of the modern world, perhaps you do not believe in complete honesty and trust. I am beginning to think that you have more in common with Anita than you care to admit. At least be honest with yourself.'

'I have done nothing these past hours but question myself, Ma. I am ashamed to face myself. But I promise I will never again hurt Ruby. Ruby's heart is a flourishing entity and has room for everything and everybody. Whereas Anita, with her empty heart, has nothing to offer. I cannot retrace my steps from Ruby's warmth and generosity to Anita's cold and calculated existence. Don't condemn me to a life in hell when heaven is so within my reach. Even God forgives all those who confess, repent and promise to reform.'

'If you understand so much, you must promise to bear in mind that to me Ruby's life is as precious a gift as yours is.'

'Ma, I know I have behaved like a greedy, obnoxious, totally deplorable cad. But I would never lie to you. You know that.'

'More than me, you need to commit yourself to Ruby. She is the one who came to you with the dream of a happy future. All the other suitors offered more financially and socially. She came to you thinking she had found a companion who understood her,' Ma shakes her head. 'I don't know how you are thinking of making it right.'

'Trust me Ma; I will never hurt her again. I promise.'

'She left for the Nilachal hill early in the morning; she wished to take a long walk.'

Ma looks at her son. Pranjal with his unshaved face and eyes exhausted due to lack of sleep made a pitiable sight. Overcome with motherly instinct; she wanted to reach out to sooth away his sorrow.

'First, go to the wash room and change. I will ring Ruby and let her know that you are here.' She did not want him to take Ruby unawares. Ruby had trusted her enough to seek refuge in her house. She would not betray the girl's trust by allowing Pranjal to assault her susceptible emotions by walking in unannounced with his little boy lost look of vulnerability.

Pranjal climbs the dark and ancient rocks, stealthily making his way towards Ruby. Eager to embrace her, yet reluctant to disturb her out of her reverie. Below the rocks, the mighty Brahmaputra flows deceptively languidly.

Ruby's body is as still as the old rocks. So intrinsically does her silhouette blend with the scenery that it appears to be one with nature. He fears that she is merely an apparition and may vanish into nothingness should he disturb her.

A loosely hanging chipped fragment disintegrates from a huge rock as Pranjal knocks his feet against it. The broken piece rolls down the slope of the rock into the river.

'It will become an independent pebble in its new surroundings. And waltz in happiness in its individuality,' Ruby says without turning around.

Pranjal sighs. He had been unconsciously holding his breath, anxious not to upset the tranquillity of the moment. He moves forward and sits by her side.

Chapter 22

'Ruby, we've been married almost three years now. I still have over twenty-five years service life left. I do not wish to waste precious energy outsmarting colleagues and seniors merely for crawling up the ladder. There is too much negativity in cut—throat competition at the office,' Pranjal says.

After a pause, when Ruby makes no effort to respond, he continues, 'Most people tend to think that their thoughts are a secret. Yet, like words and actions, which can be heard and seen, thoughts also energise our relationships and surroundings. It is impossible to maintain a healthy relationship even professionally because of the enormity of negative energy emitted by their negative thoughts.'

Ruby sits on the drawing room coach drinking a cup of coffee, gazing at him calmly. His cup of delicious South Indian filter coffee remains untouched on the side table.

'Well, say something!' Pranjal observes the manner in which she weighs her words before responding by nibbling her lips.

'Actually, as far as my knowledge goes, number one: running away never solved a problem.

'Number two: the idea is to work within the accepted system, yet remain insulated from the negative energies by consistently recharging your positive outlook until optimism becomes a habit. The picture of life is far prettier when viewed sanguinely than when pessimistically scrutinised.

'Number three: of course, we must always remain alert and analyse our actions prior to execution, deliberate upon our speech before utterance.'

Ruby smiles sarcastically as she speaks the last sentence.

'I have been thinking lately, and I don't fancy ageing in a city where the old roam around like lost souls trying to grasp a foothold to savour peace and embrace happiness for a few stolen moments in their twilight years. I don't want to suddenly wake up to the reality of old age and death and fret and fume for failing to plan for the future because I was too busy concentrating all my energies in chasing promotions,' Pranjal says.

'Ageing is as natural a phenomenon as youth. Yet our present-day society adores youth and pity the elderly for their oddity. As if, aging is a strange disease, which afflicts only a section of society. We are all to blame for this malice because we refuse to acknowledge the grace of age.'

'It is not so much the thought of growing old as the thought of retiring and having no purpose in life that scares me.' Pranjal voices the fears he has only started admitting to himself.

'You are going to retire from service when you turn sixty. Then even if you don't wish to stop living, all the official paraphernalia you enjoy as an officer will be taken away from you. But you will still have an intelligent mind and a fit body which will refuse to wither away for one or two or three or even four decades. What will you do then? Will you spend your days lamenting about lack of attention from your busy children and grandchildren and deny them a peaceful life? Or, will you, like a respectable human being continue to have a purpose in life?' Ruby asks.

'If I knew the answer, I would not be so classically confused.' Pranjal replies. So far, Pranjal was safe in his powerful grid of material security. Ever since he was a ten-year-old boy, he had been so consumed with the anxiety to establish his status that trickery, manipulation, vengeance dictated his behavioural pattern, and indeed these qualities became embedded within him and became an integral part of his nature.

'That is why we need to enhance the meaning of our lives by leading a fulfilling life. We can live a meaningful life by choosing to give it a sense of purpose. Age cannot confront us when we take the initiative of extending it a welcome in anticipation of its arrival,' elaborates Ruby, the philosopher.

'How can I 'welcome' as you put it, ageing?' he wished to know.

'Remember our visit to your ancestral village, Pranjal?' Ruby enquires.

'Yes I do.'

'Your great grandfather left the village decades back in search of a better life. Since then each generation has prospered and moved up the social ladder. Still, apart from an annual visit and building gates to commemorate the death of your family members, the family has done precious little to contribute towards the progress of the village.'

'Yeah it is like walking in the red carpet all dressed up. But with no paparazzi to click a single photograph of you,' Pranjal says. 'Many times, Ma has expressed her desire to contribute to the village Dad's grandfather left behind. Due to lack of funds, she has not been able to donate much. Being innovative, however, she has been showering them with a most precious gift—her time.

She visits the village every month and spends a week teaching the children as well as the adults to read and write.'

'What do you want me to do?' Pranjal asks Ruby wearily when Ruby does not respond.

'I don't want you to do anything.' Ruby declares, greatly emphasising the 'I'. 'Should you feel like adding a more meaningful dimension to your life, perhaps you could consider spending some time in the village?'

'And live in the hut Ma stays in?' Pranjal scoffs.

'Why not? The village is green and beautiful. The hut is clean like the other huts in the village. There is an attached modern toilet unlike many of the houses in the village.' Ruby shrugs, 'and you did mention you wished to lead a more meaningful life.'

'What would we do there?' Pranjal purposely clubs them together. Pranjal is certain that he is in no way doing anything as drastic as spending time in the village without her beside him.

'For starters, we could begin with the toilets and an effective drainage system,' Ruby replies earnestly.

'You are serious, aren't you?' Pranjal asks.

'Of course. Weren't you?' Ruby counters.

'Yes I am.' Pranjal replies hastily. 'Ruby, you know I will never again lie to you as long as I live.'

There is a pregnant pause in their conversation.

'Ruby, you do forgive me. '

'It matters little whether I forgive you or not,' Ruby says. 'What matters is whether you can remain truthful to yourself. The one person you need to be honest is to yourself. If you continue to deceive yourself, you will continue your deception lifelong. The hardest task for us is being honest with ourselves. We are so scared of delving into the real reasons of our actions that we try to camouflage our true intentions by extenuating them with a thousand superficial justifications. All the time refusing to admit the real reason because we are afraid to face the truth,' Ruby says.

'I am finally free from the selfish pursuit of fame and my endless greed for money. I have realised sacrificing our home is far too heavy a price to pay for such transient pursuits. For, at the end of the day, when everyone goes back home, I don't want to be left standing alone like an overgrown schoolboy, clutching on desperately to a bygone youth when so many good things remain waiting to be unravelled,' Pranjal declares.

Ruby remains silent.

'I shouldn't have conspired with your mother to deceive you. That is not how a marriage works,' Pranjal confesses. 'I have no wish to repeat the mistakes Dad made. And there I was hatching plots behind your back; the one person in the world I had vowed to spend my life with. I figured that if I had sunk so low as to lie to you, I had sunk the lowest any man could.'

'The saving grace is that you still have the strength to acknowledge and correct your mistakes,' Ruby says softly.

'Not without you. Never without you. I would have continued to sink unrepentant in my selfishness; if you hadn't waltzed into my life to show me how wonderful life can be even without amassing money greedily like a perennially dry sponge,' Pranjal says.

'You have a lot to thank Ma. She laid the foundation for you to build your strength of character. I was only instrumental in showing you the right direction when you choose to traverse the wrong path. So many people continue to be sucked into the whirlpool of depravity when they lack the power to probe into their conscience,' Ruby says. 'I may have prevented you from traversing the misguided path, but it is your mother who has ingrained in you the power to listen to your conscience that has helped you overcome temptation,' Ruby reverts.

'Nevertheless, you are the catalyst instrumental in my turning on a new leaf,' Pranjal says.

'Only when we have tasted helplessness and insignificance we can become one in sympathy with others,' Ruby says.

'Yeah! To quote Nietzsche: anyone who has ever built a New Heaven first found the power thereto in his own hell,' Pranjal says. 'If I am to attempt the actualisation of the litany of my dreams, I need to try and understand the minds of the people around me, those I interact with, only then can I hope to proceed ahead to my next step,' Pranjal says.

'Pain teaches us to grow into stronger individuals,' Ruby says. 'Perhaps the time we spend in the village will help us to learn more about the beauty of life.'

Although at the initial stage, Pranjal is a little uncertain about the whole project; he finds himself becoming more and more involved with the village. As the years pass by, they spend at least six weeks every year in their village.

They have founded and funded a school. They have purchased a bus for the local people to drive down to the nearby town to buy their provisions. They have even set up a store in Guwahati for them to sell their products.

Since the scenic beauty of the village is so appealing, they have constructed a tourist lodge for city dwellers to come and relax amidst the sylvan surroundings, and indulge in fresh local produce. Initially, not many venture into the village fearing undesirable elements. Happily, as satisfied visitors spread the word about this pretty spot, they find all the rooms booked months in advance.

They maintain a well-stocked library for visitors as well as for the inhabitants of the village to read. The library has developed into a community centre for people to congregate every evening.

It has become the symbol of progress, of even better times to come.

Ma starts an education programme for adults. It becomes an instant hit amongst the womenfolk. They are as eager to read the books in the library as the children and the men. The services of several retired teachers are engaged on an hourly book reading session every evening in the library. In this manner, those who cannot read are able to listen to the tales of far away lands as well.

Until now, the only books they were acquainted with were the holy books the priests read in the *namghars*—places of worship.

The readings have opened their minds to a new window of the world. A world where life styles are different, continents are different, cultures are different. Yet the most sought after human qualities remain the same—love, truth, faith, bravery—the virtues every individual in this earth desires to embody. Listening to tales written by the most creative minds in the world, they experience a subtle modification in their way of thinking as time goes by.

When the teachers read out Hindi and English literature, they make an effort to explain the content in the local language so that the adults who never had access to English medium education are able to enjoy the story. The teachers earn additional allowances to translate literature into the Assamese language for greater understanding.

Everyone is encouraged to articulate his or her opinion in the magazine that Ma published. Their inability to write is no barrier as the teachers write down their thoughts for them. This interactive medium of entertainment is a very constructive recreational pastime. As they let their minds wander without restraint, they are able to explore deep within themselves and come up with ideas and thoughts that make them cry, laugh and learn.

Visiting the village annually reminds Pranjal to be thankful for the abundance in his life. He is still working in the same organisation in Gurgaon but he no longer worries needlessly about promotions and transfers. This is because he has a worthwhile existence apart from his work at the office. These days, he is at peace with his life, his self.

'Yeah, I relax at home with Ruby. We are eagerly awaiting the arrival of the new member of our family who is growing inside Ruby everyday, enhancing the radiance of her beauty. I look forward to coming home to my wife and children, tackling everyday problems that are such an enriching part of living. I know I will never hurt my child by ignoring her with my indifference. I love her already. Something tells me our first-born will be a daughter.' Pranjal types his thoughts and emails the letter to his mother.

'Learn to rein control of your escalating material desires. So that when you start earning even an obscenely exaggerated amount, your lifestyle does not reflect only your money, rather your way of life should remain as constant as your character. That way, you will always have enough to share and give,' Ma said the year Pranjal joined service.

Pranjal had slipped and fallen into a dark abyss of greed and selfishness temporarily reigning to a halt Ma's hard work in trying to make a good man of him.

No more. With Ruby beside him showing the path towards a fruitful life, he knew life would only get better with age.

He observes that Ruby prefers to purchase most of her casual clothing from the street markets and regular stores, rather than splurge on branded apparel even when she can so well afford it.

Ruby and Pranjal make it a point to travel together as often as they can. Pranjal is too much of a poet to write factual articles required by the magazines. What he does contribute at times are couplets or entire poems to accompany the amazing photographs Ruby takes. They even put up exhibitions of these photographs. In fact, they are in great demand so the earning from their sales is also good.

It is fortunate that their creative activities complement each other's output. Ruby is as passionate about photography as Pranjal is about poetry, thus here is no question of one encroaching upon the other's work. Her work is distinctly her own just as his work bears his personal signature. By giving each other independent space, they encourage one another to grow rather than impede individual creative outpourings.

All the extra money is always welcome because it enables them to invest in their village.

With their lives falling in rhythm with their heart's desires, Pranjal spent very little time with his friends. One day Rajeev invites them to dinner.

'I'll come along with Rajvir around nine o'clock,' Pranjal responds.

'No, Rajvir will be coming with his family. You bring along your family. This is a special occasion. We are celebrating the arrival of my family to come and live with me,' Rajeev announces. 'Oh! and try to reach by eight thirty. The children have to be fed early. We can relax afterwards.'

'Sure,' Pranjal responds with a smile.

'Hi!' Ruby walks into the room. 'Have you won something? You are wearing an expression of wonderment proclaiming that you have discovered hidden treasure!'

'And I have. Rajeev has finally brought his wife and children to live with him,' Pranjal says.

'Well! Wonders never cease,' Ruby smiles.

Chapter 23

One evening, while talking to Ma over phone, Pranjal broaches the subject that had been troubling him since a long time.

'Ma, I wish you had been happy with *Deuta*.'

It felt incorrect to enjoy so wholly and sense such fulfilment when his mother had suffered all her life. She was at all times there to help; her home, always a welcoming heaven.

'Pranjal, I have often thought I should talk to you about your father. You were very young when he passed away. At times I get the feeling that you blame him for all my troubles.'

'He was never there for you when you needed him Ma.'

'Times were different, darling. We have to make allowance for the manner in which he was brought up by his mother and the unnatural importance he received being the only son in a family with seven daughters.'

'But you were his wife, Ma.'

'I was the daughter-in-law foremost. Pranjal, you have to understand that we had a traditionally arranged marriage. My duties as a daughter-in-law preceded everything else. On becoming a wife, I had to fulfil many duties. I had no one to seek guidance; for those days we were expected to behave like mature women immediately after marriage.'

'It was his duty to help you adjust in your new home.'

'No Pranjal. His childhood was different. I was aware before our marriage of his upbringing. I knew he was an immensely ambitious man. I was aware of his ruthless determination to succeed in life. I was also aware that he harboured no feelings for me. He concentrated all his energies in the pursuit of his own pleasures and so was unable to spare sympathies for another being. Yet, I went ahead with the wedding because I wanted desperately to get away from home. My step-mother was monstrous towards me.'

'Why did you never protest?'

'Society has changed so tremendously these last ten years that it is hard for me to describe accurately how difficult life was then for an unmarried woman.'

'You managed to get a job.'

'That is what helped me cling on to my self-respect.'

'*Deuta* did not respect you.' It is a statement. Pranjal knew it to be the truth.

'Pranjal, your father was not fortunate enough to be brought up to behave like one would expect a man to conduct himself. He was very child-like, used to having all his wishes being fulfilled. He saw no wrong in satisfying his demands for he never learnt to restraint control like an adult. That is why he screamed and broke things when he was angry. He threw the plateful of food if he did not find it flavourful. He drank without restraint. He left the house in a huff when he was angry instead of working out a solution,' Ma speaks softly.

Pranjal realises that Ma now feels sorry for *Deuta* for his upbringing by such an unbendingly strict and ambitious mother. Pranjal's paternal grandfather—*Koka deuta*, like all his children, was completely under her, that is *Aita*'s rigid control.

'Our being is a temple of growth—ever receptive to all the changes around us, learning, growing, embracing the natural and social changes, emerging spiritually more enlightened, ceaselessly evolving to become a better person,' Ma states.

'This is why it is so important to let life flow a natural path rather than exercise rigid control over children during their formative years. We have to remember life is a process of discovery. For this reason, it is important to give the child the freedom to explore the world around creatively. When we restrain the natural curiosity with an iron hand, we risk stunting the process of development of the child,' she elaborates. She then illustrates her point.

'Say, a child wishes to play football and his mother prohibits him from playing the game due to her own preconceived notions. That yearning of the child is likely to remain frozen in a section of his mind. Even when he is past his middle age, that desire may defrost, triggered by an event and he may venture to fulfil his childhood yearning even when physically it may not be the best thing for him.

'Your *Deuta* had an exceptionally regimented childhood. While a child should learn the importance of discipline, too much control, too much supervision stunt a child's natural growth. All his desires always lay dormant, suppressed by a mother who assumed the children would live their lives according to her computation. She calculated your *Deuta* would follow her instructions throughout his life. However, one fine day he decided that he wanted his freedom to soar and seek out the world he had not been allowed to unfold as a child. And so, even though he was a married man with a wife and a child, he left home never to return,' Ma sighed.

'He never once bothered to wipe a tear from your eyes. Not even when you were sick. Ma, you deserved more.' Pranjal chokes with emotion. The picture of his frail mother lying in the bed for almost six months with illness is still painful.

Deuta never asked her how she was faring. He was tired of *Aita* forever complain about what a lazy woman Ma had become. 'If you have to die, you have to die. Stop making everyone else miserable.' *Deuta* snapped when Ma moaned in pain when she was ill.

To Pranjal's young imagination, *Deuta*'s body appeared pumped with anger like a balloon filled with gas. As a boy, Pranjal was often tempted to prick him with a needle and let out all that resentment boiling within him. Of course, even then, Pranjal sensed that life was not so simple. Unlike deflating like a balloon, he would erupt like the Mount Vesuvius if Pranjal so much as touched him.

In fact, apart from Pranjal's maternal grandfather, who sneaked out of the house to pay her a visit once, no one from the family came by to enquire about Ma's health. It was not only by taking the prescribed medicines that she recovered, but also with her immense faith in self-healing.

'The Power above surely blessed me with the ability to wipe away my hurt. Those six months during my illness, my body suffered, yet I cannot recall any pain. Recovering from my long illness, I felt I was reborn. I felt unbelievably separated from the suffering I experienced. I discovered that I had started to value each day of my life with a detached attitude. I no longer felt an ache, a desire compelling me to strive towards a long-term goal. Each day of my being alive became a superb achievement worth celebrating,' Ma recalls.

By accepting death and not reacting to despair when she suffered, Ma learnt what it meant to die immediately without argument. She conditioned herself to die immediately of the complex contradictory existence and taught herself to live each moment intensely happy. She learnt to be as fearless of death as of life.

'I've lived long enough with death knocking on my door,' Ma makes a pathetic attempt to joke.

'Ma, you aren't that old,' Pranjal argues.

'Who said anything about growing old? I feel very young. And I am going to remain young in my own style till the day I die,' Ma laughs outright this time.

'Ma, you are too young to be talking about passing away.' Pranjal hates her discussing death. It brings back unpleasant memories of his childhood when he would hear *Deuta* and *Aita* cursing Ma, wishing her dead.

'Pranjal, I have probably spent just a little over half my allotted time in this world. I will live to be an eighty, ninety year old, don't worry. However, I wish to spend the rest of my days living life my way. I have fulfilled my obligations to my family; now allow me to serve those to whom I may be of some assistance.'

'If that's what makes you happy, Ma.'

'Don't fret Pranjal. I'm fine here' Ma says. 'Take care of yourself. And don't waste time worrying about me. I am perfectly happy!' The tinkle of her lucid laughter lingers on like a lullaby long after she disconnects the line.

The delightful resonance of her precious glee echo in the study. Crystal clear. As timeless as her for whom time no longer exists. Pranjal generally switches on the speaker mode while conversing with Ma so that he can hear her vibrant voice reverberate in the room.

The secret fount of Ma's eternal youth springs from her zest of living intensely every moment of her life. The past is as dead to her as the future. And so every moment is a fresh new beginning to value.

Yes, Pranjal can imagine she is happy in the village. Waking up to the songs of the birds as the sun blushed in like a bride, to herald a new day. Faithfully tending her vegetable field and the herb garden in the early morning hours. Teaching the children with loving firmness as she had taught him all those years ago. Educating the people to enrich their lives by inculcating simple behavioural changes, such as hygienic habits. Bringing happiness to so many people is undoubtedly making her happy. Pranjal heard her happiness dreamily eloquent in her laughter. Her simplicity is the simplicity of humility.

Afterwards, in their bedroom, Pranjal recounts his conversation with his mother to Ruby.

'She is happy,' he concludes.

'I know,' Ruby sighs.

'All my life I chased money and social status to ensure lifelong happiness. You and Ma have opened my eyes to the secret of happiness. I am a lucky man to have women like the two of you in my life.'

'You are a good son and a good husband too, Pranjal. To make a relationship successful, both partners are equally responsible,' Ruby responds.

Chapter 24

Pranjal's confident and buoyant stride heralds the fact that he is euphoric with happiness. This is not to say that he was not living a happy life earlier. He was. He learnt long ago, happiness is an unwavering status of his psyche. The difference is that whereas earlier he envisioned happiness separate from his self, these days he experiences bliss in the very act of being alive.

That is to say, happiness no longer is a favourite companion who visits him ever so often; rather it is now an integral part of him. It defines his existence. In every breath he takes, he is aware of this blissful contentment.

'How did this glorious transition come forth?' Ruby enquires.

'In retrospect, it was my conscious effort to disassociate myself from constantly analysing my socio-economic status. That day, when I ranted like a mad man voicing my fear of growing old in a city where I had no roots, that was the point in time I became free from the shackles of the suffocating fabricated world. Because that was when I learnt to abandon my fear of an uncertain future,' Pranjal replies.

'I still push myself to perform better than my best. The only difference now is that these days, I relish the challenge so much that the result becomes redundant,' he adds, 'I have learnt to love and value myself for who I am rather than wait to adore what I will become.

'You know, this worship of the present has always been the secret of Ma's happiness. She pushed herself beyond all boundaries in fulfilling her duties. She aligned her mind, heart and soul on the immediate task so that the chore became elevated beyond a responsibility to the status of an adulating prayer.' Pranjal continues. 'Ma always says the truth is that a simple heartfelt prayer is powerful enough to grant us mortals the greatest happiness.'

'The future results never agitate Ma's thoughts because she is alive to every moment of her life with unconditional devotion. For her, the present is a glorious gift,' Ruby agrees.

'I too have learnt to value each moment as a cherished reward. My ambition is no longer all consuming. Perhaps, I will not step up the promotional ladder in rapid strides. Yet I do not panic when my ruthlessly motivated colleagues refer to me as less than a successful man. I am not ready to sacrifice my family life merely to earn an elevated status in the society that will forget me the day after I leave the organization. It appears far too superfluous an existence for me to sink into, no matter how modernised a concept it is endorsed to be,' Pranjal says.

'To allow myself to fall completely crushed and consumed by the ravenousness of a career goal seems a waste of the good life I am born to enjoy,' he elaborates.

'You have reached a level of maturity even your father never did,' Ruby comments.

'Perhaps *Deuta* had his reasons for surrendering himself to an all—consuming ambition that barred him from enjoying a harmonious family life. What with a mother who regimentally controlled his mind and relentlessly badgered him on to strive harder and harder. Even when fatigue griped his body and his mind demanded rest, he did not stop because he never learnt to listen to himself. So he remained his mother's mouthpiece. Except on rare occasions when his unique individuality spurted like a natural spring, healing Ma and my hungry hearts with the joy and laughter of love.' Pranjal pauses, reminiscing those rare moments.

Those precious magical moments are what Ma still remembers of her late husband.

'He stringently limited his duties to looking after the welfare of his healthy parents and well-settled sisters. Ma had to fend for herself and look after me even when she was unwell; so as far as my memory goes, even our presence in *Deuta*'s life was a faded illusion. At times, a marriage can be a strange institution wherein the woman mutely swallows pain for the peace and welfare of the family.

'Although *Deuta* was serious about diligently performing his duties as an officer, he had an extremely casual approach towards executing his responsibilities as a husband and a father. I fail to understand how it is possible for a person to be serious about one important part of his life and completely trivialise another which is an equally important one. After all, one cannot divorce one aspect of one's being from the entirety that constitutes the character of the individual,' Pranjal concluded.

In his tryst to achieve the meaningful life, Pranjal discovers, what so many others have before him, that extreme greed, unhealthy competition, insatiable desire can push one towards a precarious end. However, making a conscious effort to give back a little of what life has showered upon one is the magic factor that balances out one's life which would otherwise result in a singularly one-dimensional existence. Sharing has that miraculous power to elevate happiness to a superlative status.

By the end of their journey recorded in this tale, all the friends learnt to waltz in happiness. Rajvir created a meaningful life by establishing an educational institution in Rajpal's memory. Rajeev brought his wife and children to live together as a family. Finally, he fulfilled his commitments of being a husband and father as well, apart from those of a son. Ma, Ruby and Pranjal had their Shangri-la in their village to dip into for extra happiness. Only Anita refused to concentrate her energies in a worthwhile pursuit of reaching out to a needy soul and moving on in life. Instead, she continued her habit of scheming and manipulating, worthlessly wasting her life for a man who belonged to another.

'I wish someone could teach Anita that craving for love from someone who loves another is a worthless pursuit,' Ruby says wistfully.

'One cannot teach other individual's lessons in leading one's life. Each one of us must stumble, falter, perhaps even fall before we can pick ourselves up, drown in self pity awhile; and then, if we have strong convictions, dust off our hurt and learn afresh to navigate the path we wish to thread,' Pranjal says.

'If I ever needed proof as validation of the fact that you have finally gained clarity of vision on the principles of ethics, you will value in your life; this statement is surely testimony enough,' Ruby smiles.